# NIGHT OF JANUARY 16TH

*A Comedy-Drama in Three Acts*

BY
AYN RAND

EDITED BY
NATHANIEL EDWARD REEID

*All Amateur Presentation*
*Rights Must be Secured*
*from the Publishers*

D0921126

DAVID McKAY COMPANY, INC.

750 THIRD AVENUE
NEW YORK, N.Y. 10017

## WARNING

# IMPORTANT INFORMATION FOR THE DIRECTOR

BECAUSE of the fundamental difference between the tasks of the player and the director, we have published a Director's Manuscript entirely separate from the Player's Book. It differs from the Player's Book in the following respects:

The Player's Book is for the actor alone. It is intended solely for his convenience in memorizing his lines and taking down the stage directions pertaining to his part. Beyond the psychology of the part, it contains no instructions whatever, and will not serve the director in producing the play.

But the Director's Manuscript is a complete producing text in every particular. It has been arranged wholly from the director's standpoint, and is intended only for his use. It contains the following additional information: Principles of acting and directing; all scene plots; property lists of each act; outline of lighting and stage effects; photographs of stage sets and characters; descriptions of characters; costumes, and make-up; and complete stage directions; reproducing utterly the entire action of the original professional performance. It is one of the most adequate play manuscripts ever offered. This Manuscript will be lent to amateurs free for the production, but must be returned immediately thereafter. It is valued at $5.00 and a corresponding charge will be made for its loss or destruction.

Prior rights of author and producer make it necessary for us to charge a royalty for the use of our plays. In all cases, this royalty will be kept as low as possible. Its payment covers the production by performance and will be quoted for any play upon application.

In ordering for production, send both the amount for royalty and the amount for as many Player's Books as the actors may wish to use, stating the dates on which the performance is to be given. Right of production will then be issued. The Player's Books may be purchased at any time. But in no circumstances will the Director's Manuscript be sent out until the royalty has been paid or guaranteed.

# NIGHT OF JANUARY 16TH

# CAST OF CHARACTERS

**NIGHT** OF JANUARY 16TH was produced by A. H. Woods at the Ambassador Theatre, New York, on September 16th, 1935 with the following

| | |
|---|---|
| PRISON MATRON . . . | *Maud Denton* |
| BAILIFF . . . . | *Donald Oliver* |
| JUDGE HEATH . . . | *J. Arthur Young* |
| DISTRICT ATTORNEY FLINT . | *Edmund Breese* |
| HIS SECRETARY . . . | *Lota James* |
| DEFENSE ATTORNEY STEVENS . | *Paul McGrath* |
| HIS SECRETARY . . . | *Eva Edwards* |
| CLERK OF THE COURT . | *George Anderson* |
| KAREN ANDRE . . . . | *Doris Nolan* |
| DR. KIRKLAND . . . | *Edward Wing* |
| MRS. JOHN HUTCHINS . . | *Calvina Thomas* |
| HOMER VAN FLEET . . . | *Harry Short* |
| ELMER SWEENEY . . . | *Leo Kennedy* |
| NANCY LEE FAULKNER . . | *Verna Hillie* |
| MAGDA SVENSON . . . | *Sarah Padden* |
| JOHN GRAHAM WHITFIELD . . | *Clyde Fillmere* |
| JANE CHANDLER . . . | *Maurie Morris* |
| SIGURD JUNGQUIST . . | *Arthur Pierson* |
| LARRY REGAN . . . | *William Bakewell* |
| ROBERTA VAN RENSSELAER . | *Marcella Swanson* |
| STENOGRAPHER . . . | *Lena Worthy* |
| POLICEMAN; 2ND POLICEMAN; COURT ATTENDANT. | |

The action of the play takes place in the Superior Court of New York City. The time is the present.

ACT I.   A day in March.
ACT II.   The next day.
ACT III.   The following **day.**

# NIGHT OF
# JANUARY 16TH

## ACT I

*The scene is the courtroom of the Superior Court of the State of New York. It faces front, so that the audience is in the position of spectators in a real courtroom. In fact, the audience must play a large part in this play, furnishing all the jury and most of the witnesses. To establish this close relationship between players and audience, the lights in the auditorium do not go out when the curtain rises.*

*At rise, the court session is ready to open, but the Judge has not made his appearance. The prosecution and defense are ready at their respective tables; the attendants are lolling about ad lib. Presently the Prison Matron brings in Karen Andre through the prison cage. All turn and look at her. The Bailiff now rises and speaks sharply.*

BAILIFF. Court attention! [*All rise quickly and stand at attention, as* JUDGE HEATH *enters in his robes and mounts the steps leading to his chair or the platform.  The* BAILIFF *speaks again.*] Superior Court Number Eleven of the State of New York.  The Honorable Judge William Heath presiding.  [*The* CLERK *raps, the* JUDGE *sits, and everybody moves quickly and silently into position. The* JUDGE *speaks.*]

JUDGE.  The people of the State of New York versus Karen Andre.

FLINT [*Rises*].  Ready, your Honor.

STEVENS [*Rises*].  Ready, your Honor.

JUDGE.  The Clerk will draw a jury.

CLERK [*Steps front with a list in his hand, and addresses the audience*].  You are the panel from which the jury will be selected to try this case. Twelve will be drawn.  As I draw your name, please answer present and step up here, take your seats and receive your instructions from Judge Heath.  [*He reads twelve names.  The jurors take their places.  When the jurors are seated, the lights in the audience go out.*]  Jurors please rise—place your hand on the Bible—raise your right hands.  [JURORS *rise.*]  Do you swear to well and fairly try this case and render a true verdict—so help you God?  Say—"I do!"

JURORS.  I do.

JUDGE HEATH [*To the jury*].  Ladies and gentlemen, you're the jurors who will try this case.  At its close you will retire to the jury room and vote upon your verdict.  I instruct you to listen to the testimony carefully and pronounce your judgment to the best knowledge of your hearts and mind.

You are to determine whether the defendant is guilty or not guilty of the murder of Bjorn Faulkner and her fate rests in your hands. The District Attorney may now proceed.

FLINT [*Rises and after a few flourishes, speaks slowly and dramatically*]. Gentlemen of the jury —on the sixteenth of January—near midnight— the body of a man came hurtling through space, and crashed—a disfigured mass—at the foot of the Faulkner Building. He was thrown, or leaped, from the roof of his luxurious penthouse. The defense will claim that it was suicide—that this great man was unwilling to bend before his creditors and acknowledge his ruin. That he found the fall from the roof of the tallest building in the world shorter and easier than the descent from the throne of the world's financial dictator. A few months ago, behind every big financial transaction in the world, stood that well known figure —with kingdoms and nations in one hand, and a whip in the other. Then why should he commit suicide? No one suspected that a gigantic swindle lay at the foundation of the Faulkner Enterprises. No one suspected that the entire business world was in danger of a heart attack. A few days after his death, the earth shook from the crash of his business. Thousands of investors were stricken with paralysis when that monstrous heart stopped beating.

Two women ruled his life—and his death. **Here** is one of them. Karen Andre—Faulkner's efficient secretary and notorious fellow swindler. But there was another, one whom fate had sent him for his salvation. This was the lovely girl who is now his widow, Nancy Lee Faulkner, only daughter of John Graham Whitfield, our great philanthropist. Faulkner thought he had found a new life in the innocence of his young bride. He was going to start all over. And the best proof of that is that two weeks after his wedding he dismissed his secretary—Karen Andre. He was through with her. But, gentlemen, one is not easily through with a woman like Karen Andre. We can only guess what hatred and revenge smouldered in her heart. No, Bjorn Faulkner did not kill himself. He was murdered, and the State contends he was murdered by the woman you see before you, Karen Andre—that on the night of January 16th she took her revenge. That, gentlemen, is what we are to prove! Our first witness will be Dr. Kirkland.

CLERK. Dr. Kirkland! [*He enters from the audience and goes to the witness chair. He has the air of a college professor. The* CLERK *offers the Bible on which all witnesses must swear.*] You solemnly swear to tell the truth, the whole truth and nothing but the truth so help you God?

KIRKLAND. I do.

FLINT. Kindly state your name.

KIRKLAND. Thomas Kirkland.

FLINT. What is your occupation?

KIRKLAND. Medical Examiner of this county.

FLINT.  In the course of your duty, what were you called upon to do on the night of January sixteenth?

KIRKLAND.  I was called to examine *the body of Bjorn Faulkner.*

FLINT.  You found a body greatly mangled by a fall?

KIRKLAND.  Yes.

FLINT.  Was that all?

KIRKLAND.  No.  A closer examination revealed a bullet wound between the fourth and fifth interspace, in the region of the heart.

FLINT.  What did you establish as the cause of death?

KIRKLAND.  It was impossible to determine.  It could have been the wound—or the fall.

FLINT.  In your opinion, could a thirty-two calibre bullet have caused the wound?

KIRKLAND.  Yes, it could.

FLINT.  How long had Faulkner been dead when you examined his body?

KIRKLAND.  I reached the body about half an hour after the fall.

FLINT.  Judging by the condition of the body, could you say exactly how long it had been dead?

KIRKLAND.  No, I could not.  Owing to the cold weather, the blood had coagulated immediately, which makes a difference of several hours impossible to detect.

FLINT.  Therefore, it is possible that Faulkner had been dead longer than half an hour?

KIRKLAND. It is possible.

FLINT. Then he could have been dead *before* he was thrown off the penthouse?

KIRKLAND. Yes.

FLINT. That is all, Doctor. [*Gives the defense a look and goes to his table.*]

STEVENS [*Rises and speaks directly to the witness*]. You said that Faulkner could have been shot and died before he fell from the penthouse, Doctor Kirkland. [KIRKLAND *nods.*] But can you state positively that he died as a *result* of that bullet wound?

KIRKLAND. No, owing to the condition of the body, it was impossible to determine.

STEVENS. Is it possible that Faulkner was conscious and able to move *after* he was wounded?

KIRKLAND. Yes, it is possible.

STEVENS. So he could have shot himself and then leaped from the building?

KIRKLAND. He could—yes—but——

STEVENS. That's all. [*Goes to his table.*]
[DR. KIRKLAND *leaves the stand a little embarrassed.*]

FLINT. Mrs. John Hutchins!

CLERK. Mrs. John Hutchins! [MRS. HUTCHINS *enters from the audience, nervously fingering her purse with both hands, and goes to the witness chair.*] You solemnly swear to tell the truth, the whole truth and nothing but the truth so help you God?

MRS. HUTCHINS. Yes, sah, I does.

FLINT. What is your name?

MRS. HUTCHINS [*Timidly*]. Mrs. John Joseph Hutchins.

FLINT. And your occupation?

MRS. HUTCHINS. I ain't got no occupation. I'se jes' the wife of my husband.

FLINT. What does your husband do?

MRS. HUTCHINS. He's the night janitor in the Faulkner Building, sah.

FLINT. Did Mr. Faulkner have business offices in that building?

MRS. HUTCHINS. Yes, sah.

FLINT. And did he have the penthouse on the roof of the building?

MRS. HUTCHINS. Yes, sah.

FLINT. And who lived there?

MRS. HUTCHINS. Mr. Faulkner did—that is, before he got married.

FLINT. And after his marriage?

MRS. HUTCHINS. After his marriage, Miss Andre lived there—all by herself.

FLINT. Have you ever seen Mr. Faulkner calling on Miss Andre after his marriage?

MRS. HUTCHINS. Yes, sah, one time.

FLINT. And that was?

MRS. HUTCHINS. On the night of January sixteenth.

FLINT. Tell us about it, Mrs. Hutchins.

MRS. HUTCHINS. Well, it was about ten thirty and——

FLINT. Just a moment. How did you know the time?

MRS. HUTCHINS. My husband always goes to work every night at ten o'clock. But on that night, I works fo' him.

FLINT. Why didn't your husband work that night?

MRS. HUTCHINS. Well, fo' the las' year or two now my husband don't seem to have no mo' gumption; and when he don't, I takes his place.

FLINT. Oh! So on the night of January 16th, your husband was low on gumption.

MRS. HUTCHINS. Yes, sah. An' it was about thirty minutes after I goes to work that the doo' bell at the private entrance rung. I went there and opened the doo'. It was Miss Andre, and Mr. Faulkner was with her. I was 'sprised, 'cause Miss Andre has her own key and, mos' times, she opens the doo' herself.

FLINT. Was she alone with Mr. Faulkner?

MRS. HUTCHINS. No, sah. There was two other gentlemen with them.

FLINT. Who were they?

MRS. HUTCHINS. I don' know, sah.

FLINT. Had you ever seen them before?

MRS. HUTCHINS. No, sah, never.

FLINT. What did they look like?

MRS. HUTCHINS. They was tall and sort of slender, both of them. One of them had his hat all crooked over his eyes and his coat collar turned up. He had been drinking.

FLINT. How do you know?

MRS. HUTCHINS. Mr. Faulkner and the other gentleman had to help him into the elevator—his feet was so loose.

FLINT. Did Mr. Faulkner look worried?

MRS. HUTCHINS. No, sah. He seemed powerful happy.

FLINT. Did he look like a man contemplating self-destruction?

MRS. HUTCHINS. Which?

FLINT. I mean did he look as if he would kill himself?

MRS. HUTCHINS. No, sah—lessen he died a-laughing.

STEVENS [*Rises*]. We object, your Honor!

JUDGE HEATH. Objection sustained.

MRS. HUTCHINS [*Frightened*]. Now what I gon' an' don'?

FLINT. Nothing at all. Just answer the questions. Did the others in the party seem happy, too?

MRS. HUTCHINS. Yes, sah. They was all laughing when they went up in the elevator—'ceptin' the drunk one.

FLINT. Did you see any of them leave, that night?

MRS. HUTCHINS. Yes, sah. The first one left about fifteen minutes later.

FLINT. Who was that?

MRS. HUTCHINS. The drunk one. He come down in the elevator, all by hisself. He didn't seem quite so drunk no more. He could walk, but he staggered a little. He still kep' his hat pulled down over his face. I wanted to help him to the doo', seeing the condition he was in, but he noticed me coming and he hurried out.

FLINT. Did you see where he went?

MRS. HUTCHINS. Yes, sah. He got into a gray coupe parked right at the entrance and he drove away fast. But the cops must've got him.

FLINT. What makes you think that?

MRS. HUTCHINS. Well, I noticed a car that started right after him.

[KAREN *comes to life, suddenly, out of her frozen calm. She jumps up and throws her question at Mrs. Hutchins.*]

KAREN. What car?

JUDGE HEATH [*Raps*]. The defendant will please keep quiet. [STEVENS *whispers to Karen, forcing her to sit down.*]

FLINT. If Miss Andre will let me do the questioning, I may satisfy her curiosity. I was just going to ask "what car," Mrs. Hutchins?

MRS. HUTCHINS. It was a big black one—a seedan, I reckon. It was parked two cars away from the first one.

FLINT. How many were in it?

MRS. HUTCHINS. I saw jus' one man.

FLINT. What makes you think he was after the first car?

MRS. HUTCHINS. Well, I couldn't be sho' he was, sah. It jus' looked funny they started together like that.

FLINT. Did you see that other guest of Miss Andre's leaving, too?

MRS. HUTCHINS.  Yes, sah.  He come down about ten minutes later.

FLINT.  What did he do?

MRS. HUTCHINS.  Nothing much.  He seemed to be in a hurry.  So he went right out.

FLINT.  And that left Mr. Faulkner and Miss Andre up in the penthouse alone?

MRS. HUTCHINS.  Yes, sah.

FLINT [*Close to witness chair*].  And then what?

MRS. HUTCHINS.  Well, I went on about my work. It must have been an hour later, when I heard screams outside in the street.  Then I saw Miss Andre running out of the private entrance, her gown all torn, sobbing wild-like.  I run after her. We pushed through the crowd outside—and there was Mr. Faulkner laying on the sidewalk all mashed to pieces.

FLINT.  What did Miss Andre do?

MRS. HUTCHINS.  She jes' screamed and fell on her knees.

FLINT.  That is all, Mrs. Hutchins.  [*Turns away*.]

MRS. HUTCHINS.  No, sah, that ain't all.  There's mo'.

FLINT.  More?  More what?

MRS. HUTCHINS.  Well, jes' then some other people come a-running up and tried to tell the policeman something.

FLINT.  What did they say?

MRS. HUTCHINS.  I don' know.

FLINT.  You don't know?

MRS. HUTCHINS. No, sah.

FLINT. What else?

MRS. HUTCHINS. Then the policeman took 'em all up to the penthouse.

FLINT. Did you go with them to the penthouse?

MRS. HUTCHINS. No, sah. Jes' as I started after them, they shet the doo'.

FLINT. Then you really don't know any more, do you?

MRS. HUTCHINS [*Embarrassed*]. Well—no, sah— now I come to think of it, I spec' I don't.

FLINT. That's all. [*She rises.*]

STEVENS. Just a moment. You said that you had never seen Mr. Faulkner calling on Miss Andre after his marriage, with the exception of that night. Now, tell me, do you always see every visitor who comes into the building at night?

MRS. HUTCHINS. No, sah. If the guest has a key to the penthouse entrance he can come in and I wouldn't see him.

STEVENS. In other words, Mr. Faulkner could have called on Miss Andre any number of times and you would not have seen him come in?

MRS. HUTCHINS. No, sah. 'Cause I don't spy on people. Whatever they does, I leaves it at that.

STEVENS. That is all. [MRS. HUTCHINS *does not move.*]

JUDGE HEATH. You may leave the chair now.

MRS. HUTCHINS. Oh! Yes, sah! [*Exits.*]

FLINT. Homer Van Fleet!

CLERK. Homer Van Fleet! [HOMER VAN FLEET

*makes his appearance, and goes to the witness
chair as if testifying were a daily routine. The*
CLERK *pokes the Bible under his nose.*] You
solemnly swear to——

VAN FLEET.  I do! [CLERK *jerks the Bible back
and gives him a look as he turns away.*]

FLINT.  Your name?

VAN FLEET.  Homer Herbert Van Fleet.  [*Fishes
in vest pocket.*]

FLINT.  Occupation?

VAN FLEET.  Private investigator.  [*Fishes out
note book.*]

FLINT.  What was your last assignment?

VAN FLEET.  Shadowing Mr. Bjorn Faulkner.
[*The Court takes notice.*]

FLINT.  By whom were you hired to do it?

VAN FLEET.  By Mrs. Bjorn Faulkner.

FLINT.  Were you shadowing Mr. Faulkner on the
night of January sixteenth?

VAN FLEET.  I was.

FLINT.  Kindly tell us about it.

VAN FLEET [*Glancing at his note book, he speaks
as if reporting to an employer*].  I start at six
thirteen P. M.  Mr. Faulkner leaves home at
Long Island.  Wears formal dress suit.  Drives
roadster himself, alone.  Unusual speed all the
way to New York.

FLINT.  Where does Mr. Faulkner go?

VAN FLEET.  He drives up to the Faulkner Building and goes in.  I wait outside, in my car.  Nine
thirty-five P. M.  Mr. Faulkner comes out with

Miss Andre. Miss Andre is wearing a corsage of orchids of unusual proportions. They drive away.

FLINT. Where do they go?

VAN FLEET. No one is perfect in this world.

FLINT. What do you mean?

VAN FLEET. I lost track of them.

FLINT. What!

VAN FLEET. Due to Mr. Faulkner's speed and an accident.

FLINT. What accident?

VAN FLEET. My left fender crashing into a truck; damages to which fender charged to Mrs. Faulkner.

FLINT. What did you do when you lost track of them?

VAN FLEET. Returned to the Faulkner Building and waited.

FLINT. When did they return?

VAN FLEET. Ten thirty P. M. exactly. A gray coupe follows them. Mr. Faulkner gets out and helps Miss Andre. While she rings the bell, Mr. Faulkner opens the door of the gray coupe; a handsome gentleman in formal clothes steps out, and together they help out a third gentleman, the latter wearing a gray overcoat. This gentleman shows signs of inebriation.

FLINT. Then what did you do?

VAN FLEET. Left my car and went into "Gary's Grill." I must explain that I always allow myself time to take nourishment every four hours while on duty. Then I sat at a window **and** watched the door of the Faulkner Building.

FLINT. What did you observe?

VAN FLEET. Nothing— [*Looks at note book.*] for fifteen minutes. Then the man in the gray overcoat—the tipsy one—comes out and starts the car—the gray coupe. Obviously in a hurry. Drives south.

FLINT. Did you see the other stranger leave?

VAN FLEET. The handsome guy?—Yes, ten minutes later. He gets into a car which stands there at the curb and drives away south.

FLINT. Have you ever seen Mr. Faulkner with these two men before?

VAN FLEET. No. First time I ever saw them.

FLINT. What did you do when they left?

VAN FLEET. I wait. Mr. Faulkner is now alone in the penthouse with Miss Andre. I'm curious— professionally. So I go up to the night club on the roof of the Brooks Building. There's an open gallery, off the dining room. You go out and you can see the Faulkner penthouse clear as day. I go out.

FLINT. Then what?

VAN FLEET. I look.

FLINT. Then what?

VAN FLEET. I yell!

FLINT [*Comes close to him*]. What do you see?

VAN FLEET. No lights. Karen Andre's white gown shimmering in the moonlight. A man in **e**vening clothes—Faulkner leaning against **the** parapet. She pushes him with all her strength. He goes over the parapet. Down—into space.

FLINT. Then what do you do?

VAN FLEET. I rush back into the dining room. Yell about what I'd seen. A crowd follows me down to the Faulkner Building. We find the bloody mess on the pavement and Miss Andre sobbing over it, fit to kill.

FLINT [*To Stevens*]. Your witness.

STEVENS [*Gets up and walks slowly toward Van Fleet, eyeing him steadily*]. Can you kindly tell us, Mr. Van Fleet, when you started in the employ of Mrs. Faulkner?

VAN FLEET. October thirteenth last.

STEVENS. Can you tell us the date of Mr. and Mrs. Faulkner's wedding?

VAN FLEET. October twelfth—the day before.

STEVENS. Exactly—just the day before. In other words, Mrs. Faulkner hired you to spy on her husband the day after their wedding?

VAN FLEET [*Undisturbed*]. So it seems.

STEVENS. What were Mrs. Faulkner's instructions when you were hired?

VAN FLEET. To watch every action of Mr. Faulkner and report in detail.

STEVENS. Had Mr. Faulkner been calling on Miss Andre after his wedding?

VAN FLEET. I don't know. He went to the Faulkner Building every day. He may have gone to his office; or he may have gone up to the penthouse; or Miss Andre may have come down to his office. I don't know what is customary.

STEVENS. Did you report *that* to Mrs. Faulkner?

VAN FLEET. I did.

STEVENS. Did she seem worried?

VAN FLEET. I don't believe so. [*He declaims in a slightly unnatural tone.*] "Mr. Faulkner was the most devoted of husbands and he loved his wife dearly."

STEVENS. Just how do you know that?

VAN FLEET [*Looking at his book*]. Those are Mrs. Faulkner's own words.

STEVENS. Now, Van Fleet, can you tell us exactly what time you started up to the night club atop of the Brooks Building on the evening of January sixteenth?

VAN FLEET. At eleven thirty-two exactly.

STEVENS. How long a walk is it from the Faulkner Building to the Brooks Building?

VAN FLEET. Three minutes.

STEVENS. What time was it when you came out on the balcony of the club?

VAN FLEET. Eleven fifty-seven.

STEVENS. So it took you exactly twenty-five minutes to get to the balcony. What were you doing the rest of the time?

VAN FLEET. Well, they have dancing at the club —and other things.

STEVENS. Did you partake of the—"other things"?

VAN FLEET. Well, I had a couple of drinks, if I

understand the drift of your curiosity. But you can't say I was intoxicated.

STEVENS. I have said nothing of the kind—as yet. Now you saw Miss Andre pushing Mr. Faulkner off the roof and it was a little distance away, in the darkness, and you were [VAN FLEET *straightens up defiantly.*]—well, shall we say you just had a couple of drinks?

VAN FLEET. The drinks had nothing to do with it.

STEVENS. Are you quite certain that she was *pushing* him? Isn't it possible that she was *struggling* with him?

VAN FLEET. Well, it's a funny way of struggling.

STEVENS. Mr. Van Fleet, what were Mrs. Faulkner's instructions to you before you came here to testify?

VAN FLEET [*With indignation*]. Mrs. Faulkner has not been here to instruct me. As everybody knows, Mrs. Faulkner and her father disappeared shortly after Faulkner's death, and have not been heard from since.

STEVENS. Have you heard from them since?

VAN FLEET. I have no record of it.

STEVENS. Mr. Van Fleet, can you tell us how much an eye witness to Mr. Faulkner's murder would be worth to Mrs. Faulkner?

FLINT [*Jumping up*]. We object, your Honor!

JUDGE HEATH. Objection sustained!

STEVENS. Exception! That's all, Mr. Van Fleet.

KAREN. Just a moment, please. Mr. Stevens——

STEVENS. Yes, Miss Andre. [KAREN *whispers to*

[ 20 ]

*Stevens.*] What kind of a car do you drive, Mr. Van Fleet?

VAN FLEET. A brown coupe—old, but serviceable. [KAREN *again whispers to Stevens.*]

STEVENS. Did you see any car following the gentleman in the gray coat when he drove away, Mr. Van Fleet?

VAN FLEET. I cannot recall. The traffic was quite heavy.

STEVENS. That's all, Mr. Van Fleet. [VAN FLEET *exits.*]

FLINT. Elmer Sweeney!

CLERK. Elmer Sweeney! [SWEENEY, *a round-faced, rookie policeman, takes the stand.*] You solemnly swear to tell the truth, the whole truth and nothing but the truth, so help you God?

SWEENEY. Yes, sir. I do.

FLINT. Your name?

SWEENEY. Elmer Sweeney.

FLINT. Your occupation?

SWEENEY. Policeman. Been in the service just a year. During that time I have caught over——

FLINT. Yes—but on the night of January sixteenth were you at the scene of Bjorn Faulkner's death?

SWEENEY. Yes, sir, right there! It had hardly happened when——

FLINT. Well—did you question Miss Andre?

SWEENEY. Not right away. Before I could do anything, that fellow Van Fleet rushed up to me and yelled how he had seen Karen Andre push Faulkner off the roof.

FLINT. How did Miss Andre react to that?

SWEENEY. She started laughing. I thought she'd went crazy.

FLINT. What did you do?

SWEENEY. I took her right up with us in the elevator—to examine the penthouse.

FLINT. Did you find anything unusual?

SWEENEY. I say I did! When we stepped out of the elevator, I thought we was in the country. Right there on the roof was a lake, with trees and grass—real trees as big around as that! [*He shows him.*] And a sandy beach—just like Coney Island!

FLINT. What was the first thing you did?

SWEENEY. Turned the shower on.

FLINT. Why did you do that?

SWEENEY. I had heard that Mr. Faulkner, when he lived there, always bathed in wine. I wanted to see if it was true.

FLINT. Was it true?

SWEENEY. If it was, the service had been discontinued.

FLINT. But did you find anything connected with Faulkner's death?

SWEENEY. Oh, that! Yes, sir. A letter in the drawing room. I saw it the moment I went in.

FLINT. Where was it?

SWEENEY. Propped up on the center table. [*There is a commotion in the courtroom.* NANCY LEE FAULKNER *enters from the audience accompanied by* WHITFIELD.]

NANCY LEE. Mr. Flint!

FLINT. Mrs. Faulkner! [*To Judge*] Your Honor, please, this is a witness I have been trying to locate.

JUDGE HEATH. Very well! [KAREN *jumps up. A silent, significant exchange of looks between the two women.* STEVENS *forces Karen to sit down.*]

FLINT. We have searched everywhere for you, Mrs. Faulkner.

NANCY LEE. I went to California for a quiet rest. But I saw in the papers that you wanted to call me as a witness and I hurried back. Father brought me here by airplane. I want to do my duty toward the—memory of my husband.

WHITFIELD [*Shakes hands with* FLINT]. If there is anything we can do to help you, Mr. Flint, we're at your disposal.

FLINT. I can only express my deepest appreciation, Mr. Whitfield. If you will kindly take seats, I will be ready for you in just a little while. No, sit in this chair. [*Leads them to prosecution table and offers Nancy a chair facing the jury.*]

STEVENS [*Jumping up*]. We object, your Honor! This is an attempt to influence the jury! A trick to make them face Mr. Faulkner's widow throughout the trial!

FLINT. Your Honor, the defense counsel has no right to dictate where I seat my witnesses.

JUDGE HEATH. Silence! I shall allow it. Objection overruled.

FLINT [*Resumes the examination of Sweeney*]. A moment ago, you said you found a letter.

SWEENEY. Yes, sir—in the drawing room.

FLINT [*Showing him a letter*]. Is this the letter?

SWEENEY. Yes—the very same. How did you get it?

FLINT. Please, read it to the jury?

SWEENEY [*Reading*]. "If any future historian wants to record my last advice to humanity, I'll say that I found only two valuable things on this earth: My whip over the world and Karen Andre. To those who can use it, the advice is worth what it has cost mankind. Bjorn Faulkner."

FLINT [*Hands it to Clerk*]. Submitted as evidence.

JUDGE HEATH. Accepted as Exhibit A.

FLINT. Was that all you found?

SWEENEY. I should say not! Out on the roof garden I found a gun. It was about that long and——

FLINT [*Taking gun from desk*]. I will now show you a thirty-two calibre pistol. Is this the weapon you found?

SWEENEY [*Takes gun*]. The very same! So you got hold of that too!

FLINT. Submitted as evidence.

JUDGE HEATH. Accepted Exhibit B.

FLINT. Where did you find it?

SWEENEY. It was lying under a chair. I picked up the gun with my handkerchief—I always watch out for finger prints. The barrel smelled strongly of powder, which showed that it had just been fired.

FLINT.  Did you ask Miss Andre whose gun it was?

SWEENEY.  Yes, sir.  She said it was hers.

FLINT [*Turns to Karen*].  How did she explain the shot?

SWEENEY.  She said that Faulkner had been un‑happy; that he wrote the letter and left it there in the drawing room and ordered her not to touch it.  Then he opened a drawer and grabbed this gun.  She saw what he was going to do and struggled with him.  In the struggle, the gun went off and Mr. Faulkner was wounded in the chest.

FLINT.  Miss Andre told you that the gun was in Faulkner's hand when it went off?

SWEENEY.  Yes, sir.

FLINT.  She was positive about it?

SWEENEY.  Said it three times.

FLINT.  Was the gun examined for finger prints?

SWEENEY.  Sure—at headquarters—here are the photographs.

FLINT.  And were the police able to identify them?

SWEENEY.  They were exactly like these, sir.

FLINT.  And whose are these?

SWEENEY.  Karen Andre's.

FLINT.  And did that gun show any finger prints other than Karen Andre's?

SWEENEY.  Not a one.

FLINT [*Gives them to Clerk*].  Submitted as evidence.

JUDGE HEATH.  Accepted.  Exhibits C and D.

FLINT. Now, after the gun went off in Faulkner's hand, what happened next, according to Miss Andre?

SWEENEY. She said Faulkner dropped the gun and yelled that she couldn't stop him, and before she knew it, he had leaped off the roof.

FLINT. Did you ask her who had been with them that night?

SWEENEY. Yes, sir, I did. She said two gentlemen had: that they were friends of Mr. Faulkner and that she had met them for the first time that evening while eating dinner with Faulkner.

FLINT. And Miss Andre told you that she had never seen these two men before?

SWEENEY. Yes, sir.

FLINT. Was she very emphatic about that?

SWEENEY. Yes, sir—couldn't shake her.

FLINT. That is all.

STEVENS. Miss Andre told you that she had struggled with Faulkner to prevent his suicide. Did you notice any evidence of a struggle in her clothes?

SWEENEY. Yes, sir. Her dress was tore. It had diamond straps, and one of them was broke, so that she had to hold the dress up with one hand. I was so embarrassed!

STEVENS. That's all. [SWEENEY *exits.*]

FLINT. Jane Chandler!

CLERK. Jane Chandler! You solemnly swear to tell the truth, the whole truth and nothing but the truth so help you God?

MISS CHANDLER.  I do!

FLINT.  Your name!

MISS CHANDLER.  Jane Chandler.

FLINT.  Your occupation?

MISS CHANDLER.  Handwriting expert of the New York Police Department.

FLINT [*Taking letter from Clerk*].  Exhibit A. Please—do you recognize this letter?

MISS CHANDLER [*Examines letter*].  Yes. I understand it is a letter found in Mr. Faulkner's penthouse the night of his death.  I had been called upon to examine it.

FLINT.  What were you asked to determine?

MISS CHANDLER.  I was asked to determine whether it was written by Mr. Faulkner.

FLINT.  What is your verdict?

MISS CHANDLER.  Certain peculiarities in the handwriting lead me to the conclusion that this letter was forged.  [FLINT *returns letter to Clerk*.]

FLINT [*To Stevens*].  Your witness.

STEVENS.  Miss Chandler, it was called to your attention during the inquest that Miss Andre was in the habit of signing Faulkner's name to unimportant documents at the time she was employed as his secretary.  Have you compared these signatures with Faulkner's real ones?

MISS CHANDLER.  I have.

STEVENS.  What is your opinion of them?

MISS CHANDLER.  I can compliment Miss Andre on her art.  The difference is very slight.

STEVENS.  Bearing that in mind, isn't it impossible

to tell the difference between Faulkner's real handwriting and Miss Andre's imitation?

MISS CHANDLER. It is a very difficult task, but we have means of determining the difference.

STEVENS. What are the means?

MISS CHANDLER. Well, one is the microscope, which reveals certain vibrations and certain shadings of the pen, according to the nerve condition of the writer, which cannot be imitated.

STEVENS. How often are you handwriting experts wrong in your decisions?

FLINT [*Rises*]. I object, your Honor!

STEVENS. If your Honor please! This is a perfectly legitimate question, I wish to establish that this is not an exact science.

FLINT. Your Honor, this has been accepted as an exact science by all courts for a number of years, and if this lawyer doesn't know that——

JUDGE HEATH [*Raps*]. Order, gentlemen! I will sustain the objection.

STEVENS. Miss Chandler, in view of the similarity of their writing, isn't there a reasonable doubt that this letter was a forgery?

MISS CHANDLER. Of course there can be a doubt, but——

STEVENS. That's all!

MISS CHANDLER. Thank you. [*Exits.*]

FLINT. Mrs. Faulkner! [*There is a little hush of expectancy, as all eyes turn to Nancy Lee Faulkner.*]

CLERK. Mrs. Faulkner! [NANCY LEE *rises and*

*walks to the stand.*]   You solemnly swear to tell the truth, the whole truth and nothing but the truth so help you God?

NANCY LEE.   I do.

FLINT.   What is your name?

NANCY LEE.   Nancy Lee Faulkner.

FLINT.   What relation were you to the late Bjorn Faulkner?

NANCY LEE [*Faintly*].   I was—his wife.

FLINT.   When did you first meet Bjorn Faulkner?

NANCY LEE.   In August of last year.

FLINT.   Where did you meet him?

NANCY LEE.   At a ball given by a friend of mine in Newport.

FLINT [*Pauses*].   You have heard about Bjorn Faulkner's reputation as the most ruthless of men. Did you find him so on your first meeting?

NANCY LEE.   Not at all.   He was perfectly charming and considerate—that first night I met him. You see, he told me later that I was the first woman he had ever met whom he could—respect.

FLINT.   When did you see Mr. Faulkner again?

NANCY LEE.   About three weeks later.   I invited him to dine at my home on Long Island; just an informal little dinner, with father present.

FLINT.   Did you see him often after that?

NANCY LEE.   Yes, quite often.   His visits became more and more frequent until the day——  [*Her voice breaks.*]

FLINT.   Until the day?

NANCY LEE [*Her voice is hardly above a breathless whisper*]. The day he proposed to me.

FLINT. Please continue.

NANCY LEE. We went driving, Mr. Faulkner and I, alone. We stopped on a lonely little road. [*Her voice trembles, she is silent for a second. She resumes her testimony.*] I'm sorry. It's a little hard for me to think of—those days. Then suddenly Mr. Faulkner seized my hand and looking straight at me, said " I love you, Nancy." [*Her voice breaks into a sob.*]

FLINT. I'm so sorry, Mrs. Faulkner. If you wish to be dismissed now and continue tomorrow——

STEVENS [*Jumping up*]. Why, this is a subterfuge, staged to gain the sympathy of the jury!

FLINT. I object to that remark!

STEVENS. I demand a fair trial for my client, and——

FLINT. Demand what you like—there will be no interference with my witnesses!

JUDGE HEATH. Order, gentlemen! The jury will ignore these remarks. [STEVENS *sits*.]

FLINT. I am sorry, Mrs. Faulkner, for this interruption. Please proceed.

NANCY LEE. Then Mr. Faulkner told me for the first time the truth about his fortune—that it was gone. He said that he could not ask me to marry him because he had nothing to offer me. But I— I loved him. I told him that his money meant nothing to me.

FLINT.  Did Mr. Faulkner feel hopeless about the future?

NANCY LEE.  No, not at all.  I told him that it was our duty to save his enterprises—our duty to the widows and children whose savings had been entrusted to him.  He said my faith in him was like a great driving force propelling him onward —that he could not fail.  How could he think of suicide!

FLINT.  Did you remain in New York after your wedding?

NANCY LEE.  Yes.  We made our home in my Long Island residence.  Mr. Faulkner gave up his New York penthouse.

FLINT.  Did Mr. Faulkner tell you anything about Miss Andre?

NANCY LEE.  Not then.  But two weeks after our wedding, he came to me and said, " Dearest, I feel that I must tell you about the secretary who has served me so long."  I said, " You don't have to say a word if you don't want to."  He said, " I must.  My marriage to you has become a sacred troth that has regenerated my soul—and the past can have no part in it."  Then he said, " Karen Andre is the cause and symbol of my darkest years.  I am going to dismiss her."

FLINT.  What did you answer?

NANCY LEE.  I said, " We must not be cruel.  Per-haps you can find another position for Miss Andre."  He said that he'd provide for her finan-cially, but that he never wanted to see her again.

FLINT. Tell me, what did Mr. Faulkner do on the day of January sixteenth?

NANCY LEE. He spent it in town, on business, as usual. He came home late in the afternoon. He said that he had to dine with three friends that night. It was a business deal. So he did not have dinner at home. He left about six o'clock.

FLINT. Who were the three friends?

NANCY LEE. He did not tell me and I didn't ask. I made it a point never to interfere with his business.

FLINT. Did you notice anything peculiar when he said good-bye to you, that night?

NANCY LEE. No, not a thing. He kissed me good-bye and said that he'd try to come home early. I followed him to the door and watched him drive away. I stood there for a few minutes thinking how happy we were—what a perfect dream our love had been—a beautiful, uplifting relationship based on mutual trust. [*Her voice trembles.*] How could I know that this love—through jealousy—would bring about his—his death.

STEVENS [*Rises*]. Your Honor! We object! Move that be stricken out!

JUDGE HEATH. The witness' last sentence may go out.

FLINT. Thank you, Mrs. Faulkner. That is all.

STEVENS [*Rises*]. Will you be able to answer a few questions now, Mrs. Faulkner?

NANCY LEE [*Raising her tear-stained face*]. As many as you wish, Mr. Stevens.

STEVENS [*Softly*]. You said your romance was like a perfect dream, didn't you?

NANCY LEE. Yes.

STEVENS. "A sacred troth that regenerated a soul?" "A beautiful, uplifting relationship based on mutual trust?"

NANCY LEE. Yes.

STEVENS [*Fiercely*]. Then why did you hire a detective to spy on your husband?

NANCY LEE [*A little flustered*]. Why I—I didn't hire a detective to spy on my husband. I hired him to protect Mr. Faulkner.

STEVENS. Protect him? Will you kindly explain that?

NANCY LEE. Well—you see—some time ago, Mr. Faulkner had been threatened by a gangster—Larry Regan. He refused to pay any attention to it. But I was worried. So as soon as we were married, I hired Mr. Van Fleet to watch him. I did it secretly, because I knew that Mr. Faulkner would object.

STEVENS. How could a detective following at a distance protect Mr. Faulkner?

NANCY LEE. Well, I didn't think that the underworld would dare attack a man who was constantly watched.

STEVENS. So all Mr. Van Fleet had to do was to watch Mr. Faulkner?

NANCY LEE. Yes.

STEVENS. Mr. Faulkner alone?

NANCY LEE. Yes.

STEVENS. Not Mr. Faulkner *and* Miss Andre?

NANCY LEE. Mr. Stevens, that supposition is insulting to me!

STEVENS. I haven't noticed *you* sparing insults, Mrs. Faulkner.

NANCY LEE. I'm very sorry, Mr. Stevens. I can assure you that I intended no such thing.

STEVENS. You said that Mr. Faulkner told you he never wanted to see Miss Andre again?

NANCY LEE. Yes, he did.

STEVENS. And yet, after your marriage he gave her his penthouse—the most luxurious apartment in New York City. Your detective told you that, didn't he?

NANCY LEE. Yes. I knew it.

STEVENS. How do you explain it?

NANCY LEE. I cannot explain it. How can I know what blackmail she was holding over his head? [KAREN *slaps the table.*]

STEVENS. How do you explain the fact that Mr. Faulkner lied to you about dining with three friends on the night of January sixteenth and instead went directly to Miss Andre's house?

NANCY LEE. If I could explain that, Mr. Stevens, I might be able to save you the bother of this trial. We would have an explanation of my husband's death. All I know is that she had made him come to her house for some reason which he could not tell me—and that he was found dead that night.

STEVENS. That's all, Mrs. Faulkner. [NANCY LEE *rises.*]

KAREN [*Rises*]. Your Honor! May I ask her a question?

JUDGE HEATH. Granted.

KAREN. Did you love Bjorn Faulkner?

NANCY LEE. I did, Miss Andre.

KAREN. Then how can you speak of him as you did? Don't you know why he married you? [JUDGE *raps*. FLINT *rises.*] But your Honor please! [*To Nancy Lee*] How can you sit there and lie about him because he can't come back to defend himself? [JUDGE *raps*. STEVENS *goes to Karen.*]

NANCY LEE. Your Honor! Why should I be questioned by the woman who murdered my husband!

KAREN. Mrs. Faulkner!

NANCY LEE [*Stops. They are now face to face*]. What is it?

KAREN. One of us is lying—and we both know which one.

JUDGE HEATH [*Raps*]. Court will now adjourn until ten o'clock tomorrow morning.

[*As* CURTAIN *falls* STEVENS *escorts* KAREN *down to Prison Matron.*]

CURTAIN

# ACT II

*Same scene as Act I.   As the curtain rises, the Prison Matron brings in Karen.   The Bailiff speaks.*

BAILIFF.   Court attention!   [JUDGE HEATH *enters. Everybody rises.*]   Superior Court Number Eleven of the State of New York.   The Honorable Judge William Heath presiding.   [JUDGE HEATH *sits, the* CLERK *raps, and everybody resumes his seat.*]

JUDGE HEATH.   The People of the State of New York versus Karen Andre.

FLINT [*Rises*].   Ready, your Honor.

STEVENS [*Rises*].   Ready, your Honor.

JUDGE HEATH.   The District Attorney may proceed.

FLINT.   Magda Svenson!

CLERK.   Magda Svenson!   [MAGDA SVENSON *pounds down the aisle of the auditorium as if she wore wooden shoes.   She mounts the steps noisily and walks rapidly with long strides to the witness stand.*]   You solemnly swear to tell the truth, the whole truth and nothing but the truth so help you God?

MAGDA.   I svear.   [*Kisses the Bible quickly.   She speaks with Swedish accent in a loud raucous voice.*]

FLINT.  What is your name?

MAGDA.  You know it.  You yus' call me.

FLINT.  Kindly answer my questions without **argu-ment**.  State your name.

MAGDA.  Magda Svenson.

FLINT.  What country did you come from?

MAGDA.  A Svede never come from any country but Sveden.

FLINT.  What is your occupation?

MAGDA.  I bane housekeep-er.

FLINT.  By whom were you employed last?

MAGDA.  By Herr Bjorn Faulkner—and before that by his fath-er.

FLINT.  How long have you been employed by them?

MAGDA.  I bane in the family thirty-eight year. I remember Herr Bjorn since he was a little kint.

FLINT.  When did you come to America?

MAGDA.  I bane here five year.

FLINT.  What were the duties Mr. Faulkner assigned to you?

MAGDA.  I keep penthouse for him.  I stay even after he go—when he get married and give penthouse to her.  [*She points at Karen with undisguised hatred.*]  But I never employed by this one.

FLINT.  Now, *Mrs.* Svenson, what——

MAGDA [*Offended*].  *Miss* Svenson.

FLINT.  I beg your pardon, Miss Svenson.

MAGDA [*Loud singsong*].  Dass all right.

[ 37 ]

FLINT. What did you know about Miss Andre's connections with Mr. Faulkner?

MAGDA [*With forceful indignation*]. Decent voman like me shouldn't know about such tings! But sin is shameless in this vorld.

FLINT [*Comes close to her*]. Tell us about it.

MAGDA [*Jerks away from him, then speaks*]. From wery first day this voman come, she try to get her claws on Herr Faulkner. It is not good ting vhen secretary forgets to secretary.

FLINT. You mean she was in love with Faulkner?

MAGDA. Only the heart can love. She have no heart. No, she vant to know too much about Herr Faulkner's business.

FLINT. Was Faulkner in love with her?

MAGDA. He married to the other voman? A good man never loves double. Phiff!

FLINT. Then why did Faulkner insist on keeping her?

MAGDA. Before he know it, she learn so much about his business, he cannot let her go. And vhen she know she got her claws on him, she make him spend much money on her. You try to count up all money he vaste on that voman.

FLINT. Can you give any instances of his extravagance?

MAGDA. I can so. He had platinum gown made for her. Yes, I said platinum! Fine mesh—fine and soft as silk. And she vore it on her naked body. She had a fire in the fireplace, and she heated the dress. And she asked me to put it on her as hot as she could stand; and if it burned her shameless skin, she laugh like the pagan she is and say it vas man, kissing her vild like tiger.

STEVENS [*Rises*]. Your Honor, we object.

FLINT [*Enjoying himself*]. These are facts pertaining to the vital questions of this case.

STEVENS. But your Honor——

JUDGE. Silence, gentlemen! I shall ask the witness to word her testimony more modestly.

MAGDA. Sin is sin, Judge, any name you call it.

FLINT. How did Mr. Faulkner act at the time of his marriage to Miss Whitfield?

MAGDA. He vas happy for first time in his life. He vas happy like decent man vhat found right road.

FLINT. Did you know of anything that made him worry in those days, that could bring him to suicide eventually?

MAGDA. No. Nothing.

FLINT. Now, tell us, Miss Svenson, what was Miss Andre's attitude toward the other woman?

MAGDA. She silent, like stone spinx. But I hear her crying one night, after marriage. Crying, sobbing—and that the first only time in her life.

FLINT. Why was she crying?

MAGDA. I not know. All vomen cry some time— yust to cry.

FLINT. Was she crying because she had lost Faulkner?

MAGDA. No, not her! If she lose vun man, she

find another. I seen her kissing another man on the same night of Herr Faulkner's vedding.

FLINT. What man?

MAGDA. I not know the man. I seen him first time the night of Herr Faulkner's vedding.

FLINT. Tell us about it.

MAGDA. I gone to vedding. Ah, it vas beautiful. My poor Herr Bjorn so handsome, and the young bride all vhite and lovely as lily. I cried like looking at my own children. [*She bellows comically and then points at Karen ferociously.*] But *she* not go to vedding!

FLINT. Well, did Miss Andre stay at home?

MAGDA. She stay home. I come back from vedding early. I come in servants' door. She not hear me. She vas home all right. But she vas not alone.

FLINT. Who was with her?

MAGDA. *He* vas—*the man.* Out on the roof, in the garden, I see them. He held her in his arms and kiss her—the sinner!

FLINT. And then?

MAGDA. She step aside and say something. I not hear, she speak wery soft. He not say vord. He yust take her hand and hold it, and hold it so long—I get tired vaiting and go back to my room.

FLINT. Did you see the man leave?

MAGDA. No, I did not.

FLINT. Did you see him again?

MAGDA. Yes. Vunce.

FLINT. And when was that?

MAGDA. The night of Yanuary sixteenth. [*A movement in the courtroom.*]

FLINT [*Urges her saucily*]. Tell us about it, Miss Svenson.

MAGDA [*Adjusts herself cheerfully as if to tell a spicy story*]. Vell, she very strange that day. She call me and said I haf the rest of day off. And I bane suspicious.

FLINT. Why did that make you suspicious?

MAGDA. It vas Vednesday and my day off is T'ursday and I not asked for second day. So I said I not need day off, but she said she not need me. So I go.

FLINT. What time did you go?

MAGDA. 'Bout four o'clock. But I vant know secret. I koom back. [*She sings this last sentence gleefully.*]

FLINT [*Teasing her*]. When did you " koom " back?

MAGDA. 'Bout ten at night. The house dark— she not home. So I vait. Half hour after, I hear them koom. I seen Herr Faulkner with her. So I afraid to stay. But before I go I seen two gentlemen with them. Vun gentleman, oh, he drunk!

FLINT. Who was he?

MAGDA. I not know him.

FLINT. Did you know the other one?

MAGDA. The other vun—he same man I seen kiss-ing Miss Andre on vedding night.

FLINT [*Almost triumphant*]. That's all, Miss Svenson. [MAGDA *is about to leave the stand.* STEVENS *stops her.*]

STEVENS [*Rises*]. Just a minute, Miss Svenson. You still have to have a little talk with me.

MAGDA [*Resentfully*]. Ah, for vhat? I say all I know.

STEVENS. You may know the answers to a few more questions. For instance, you stated that you had seen the stranger making love to Miss Andre.

MAGDA. Yes, I did so.

STEVENS. But you also stated you could not hear what was said. Now remember, you are under oath. If you couldn't hear them, you can't really swear that he *did* make love to her, can you?

MAGDA. No-o. But I can't svear that he *didn't*, eider.

STEVENS. Can you really swear you saw him kiss her?

MAGDA. With my own two eyes I saw the sinner do it.

STEVENS. Well, after all, what is so sinful about a boy kissing a girl?

MAGDA. Listen, mister, maybe you don't know. Maybe you are too young to be experienced. But *I* know that a kiss is last door in heaven before a girl falls into hell. [*There is commotion in the courtroom. The* JUDGE *raps.*]

STEVENS. Let's confine ourselves to this case. Now, you said it was dark when you saw him for the first time?

MAGDA.    Yas, it vas dark.

STEVENS.    And, on the night of January sixteenth, when you were so ingenuously spying on your mistress, you said that you saw her come in with Mr. Faulkner, and you hurried to depart in order not to be caught.    Am I correct?

MAGDA.    You haf good memory.

STEVENS.    You just had a swift glance at the two gentlemen with them?

MAGDA.    Yes.

STEVENS.    Can you tell us what the drunken gentleman looked like?

MAGDA.    How can I?    No time to notice face and too dark at door.

STEVENS.    So!    It was too dark to identify the drunken man, and yet you were able to identify the other man you had seen but once before?

MADGA [*Slowly, with all the strength of her righteous indignation*].    Let me tell you, mister!    I'm under oat' as you say, and I'm religious voman and respect oat'.    I said it vas same man—and I say it again!    Vat do you tink—I know nothing about men?

STEVENS.    That is all.    Thank you, Miss Svenson. [*She pounds off stage hurriedly.*]

FLINT.    If your Honor please, the prosecution has one more witness to introduce.    Mr. John Graham Whitfield!

CLERK.    John Graham Whitfield!    [WHITFIELD, *seated on stage, goes to witness chair.*]    You

solemnly swear to tell the truth, the whole truth
and nothing but the truth so help you God?

WHITFIELD.   I do.

FLINT.   What is your name?

WHITFIELD.   John Graham Whitfield.

FLINT.   What is your business, or rather your occu‑
pation?

WHITFIELD.   I am president of the Whitfield Na‑
tional Bank.

FLINT.   Were you related to the late Bjorn Faulk‑
ner?

WHITFIELD.   I was his father-in-law.

FLINT.   It is obvious, Mr. Whitfield, that you are
well qualified to pass judgment on financial mat‑
ters.   Can you tell us about the state of Mr.
Faulkner's business immediately preceding his
death?

WHITFIELD.   I should say it was desperate, but not
hopeless.   My bank made a loan of twenty-five
million dollars to Mr. Faulkner in an effort to
save his enterprises.   Needless to say, that money
is lost.

FLINT.   What prompted you to make that loan,
Mr. Whitfield?

WHITFIELD.   He was the husband of my only
daughter; her happiness has always been para‑
mount to me.   But my motives were not entirely
personal.   Realizing the countless tragedies of
small investors that the crash would bring, I felt
it my duty to make every possible effort to prevent
it.

FLINT. Is it possible that you would have risked such a considerable sum in Faulkner's enterprises if you believed them hopelessly destined to crash?

WHITFIELD. Certainly not. It was a difficult undertaking, but I felt that the crash could have been prevented—had Faulkner lived.

FLINT. He therefore had no reason to commit suicide as far as his business affairs were concerned?

WHITFIELD. He had every reason for remaining alive.

FLINT. Now, Mr. Whitfield, can you tell us whether Mr. Faulkner was happy in his family life, in his relations with your daughter?

WHITFIELD. Mr. Flint, I would like to state that I have always regarded the home and the family as the most important institutions in our lives. You, therefore, will believe me when I tell you how important my daughter's happiness was to me—and she had found perfect happiness with Mr. Faulkner.

FLINT. Mr. Whitfield, what did you know about Mr. Faulkner personally?

WHITFIELD. Well, it is only fair to admit that he had many qualities of which I could not approve. We were as unlike as two human beings could be! I believe in one's duty to others above all; Bjorn Faulkner believed in nothing but himself.

FLINT. From your knowledge of him, Mr. Whitfield, would you say you consider it possible that Mr. Faulkner committed suicide?

WHITFIELD. I consider it absolutely impossible.

FLINT. Thank you, Mr. Whitfield. That is all.

STEVENS. Mr. Whitfield, were you very fond of your son-in-law?

WHITFIELD. Yes.

STEVENS. And you never disagreed with him, never lost your temper in a quarrel?

WHITFIELD [*With a tolerant smile*]. Mr. Stevens, I don't lose my temper.

STEVENS. If my memory serves me right, there was some kind of trouble at the time you made that stupendous loan to Mr. Faulkner.

WHITFIELD. Purely a misunderstanding, I assure you.

STEVENS. Oh!—

WHITFIELD. I must admit that Mr. Faulkner made—a somewhat unethical attempt to hasten that loan, which was quite unnecessary, since I granted it gladly—for my daughter's sake.

STEVENS. You said that your fortune had been badly damaged by the Faulkner crash?

WHITFIELD. Yes.

STEVENS. And your financial situation is rather strained at present?

WHITFIELD. Yes.

STEVENS. Then how could you afford to offer a twenty-five thousand dollar reward for the arrest and conviction of Larry Regan?

FLINT [*Rises*]. Objection! What has that to do with the case?

WHITFIELD. Your Honor. I would like to have the privilege of explaining this.

JUDGE. Very well.

WHITFIELD. I did offer such a reward. The gentleman commonly known as Larry Regan is a notorious criminal who specializes in extorting money for so-called " protection." He had not only menaced Mr. Faulkner, but also threatened to kidnap my daughter. I offered that reward for evidence that would make his arrest and conviction possible.

STEVENS. Mr. Whitfield, can you tell us why you and your daughter disappeared so suddenly shortly after the night of January sixteenth?

WHITFIELD. I think the answer is obvious. My daughter was crushed by the sudden tragedy. I hastened to take her away, to save her health.

STEVENS. You love your daughter profoundly?

WHITFIELD. Yes.

STEVENS. You have always made it a point that her every wish should be granted?

WHITFIELD. I can proudly say " yes."

STEVENS. When she—or you—desire anything, you don't stop at the price, do you?

WHITFIELD. Well, Mr. Stevens, we've never had to——

STEVENS. Then would you refuse to buy her the man she wanted?

WHITFIELD [*Outraged*]. Mr. Stevens!

STEVENS [*Pursuing the subject furiously*]. You wouldn't stop if it took your entire fortune to break the first unbreakable man you'd ever met?

FLINT [*Rises*]. Your Honor! We object!

JUDGE HEATH. Sustained.

STEVENS [*Still rapid*]. Exception! Now, Mr. Whitfield, perhaps you will tell us that your money had nothing to do with Mr. Faulkner dismissing Miss Andre? That no ultimatum was delivered to him?

WHITFIELD [*His tone is less composed than before*]. You are quite mistaken in your insinuation. My daughter was not in the least jealous of Miss Andre.

STEVENS. I'd be careful of statements like that, Mr. Whitfield. Remember that your daughter was elevated to the high state of matrimony by purchase.

FLINT [*Rises*]. Your Honor! We—— [JUDGE HEATH *raps his gavel; but to no avail.* NANCY LEE FAULKNER *jumps up.*]

NANCY LEE. Father! Father!

WHITFIELD. Why you—you impudent upstart— you—— Do you know that I can crush you like a worm— [JUDGE *raps.*] as I have crushed many a better——

STEVENS [*Pauses. With insulting calm*]. That is just what I wanted to prove. Thank you, Mr. Whitfield. That is all.

FLINT. Your Honor! We move that the defense counsel's outrageous remark which led to this incident be stricken out!

JUDGE HEATH. The remark may go out. [WHITFIELD *leaves the stand in ill humor.*]

FLINT [*Loud, solemn*]. The people rest.

STEVENS.   Move that the case be dismissed for lack of evidence.

JUDGE HEATH.   Denied.

STEVENS.   Exception! [*Goes to jury box.*]   Gentlemen of the jury!   We cannot pass judgment on Karen Andre without passing it on Bjorn Faulkner.   He had put himself outside all human standards.   Whether it was below or above them, is a question for each of us to decide personally. But I'll ask you to remember that he was the man who said he needed no reasons for his actions: *he* was the reason—the man who said that laws were made for the weak; that the strong were the laws. If you'll remember that, you will understand that the financial condition into which he was thrown in his last months was so intolerable to him that in order to escape it, he would resort to the most desperate means—including suicide!   And that is what the defense will prove.   [STEVENS *pauses, then calls.*]   Our first witness will be—Sigurd Jungquist!

CLERK.   Sigurd Jungquist!   [JUNGQUIST *enters from the audience and takes the stand timidly. He is Swedish and speaks with an accent.*]   Do you solemnly swear to tell the truth, the whole truth and nothing but the truth so help you God?

JUNGQUIST.   I do.

STEVENS.   What is your name?

JUNGQUIST.   Sigurd Yungquist.

STEVENS.   What is your occupation?

JUNGQUIST. My last yob was secretary to Herr Bjorn Faulkner.

STEVENS. How long have you held that job?

JUNGQUIST. Since beginning of November—since Miss Andre left.

STEVENS. What was your position before that?

JUNGQUIST. Bookkeeper for Herr Faulkner.

STEVENS. How long did you hold that job?

JUNGQUIST. Five years. [BAILIFF *leaves the room.*]

STEVENS. Did Mr. Faulkner give you Miss Andre's position when she was dismissed?

JUNGQUIST. Yes.

STEVENS. Did Miss Andre instruct you in your new duties?

JUNGQUIST. Yes, she did.

STEVENS. What was her behavior at that time? Did she seem to be angry, sorry or resentful?

JUNGQUIST. No. She was wery calm, like always, and explained everything clear.

STEVENS. Did you notice any trouble between Miss Andre and Mr. Faulkner at that time?

JUNGQUIST [*With a kind, but superior tolerance*]. Herr Lawyer, there can be no more trouble between Herr Faulkner and Miss Andre as between you and your shadow.

STEVENS. Now tell me have you ever witnessed any business conference between Mr. Faulkner and Mr. Whitfield?

JUNGQUIST. I never been present at conferences, but I see Herr Whitfield come to our office many times. Herr Whitfield he not like Herr Faulkner. [BAILIFF *re-enters with note, which he gives to* STEVENS, *who stops to read it.*]

STEVENS [*To Judge*]. Just a moment, if your Honor pleases, I would like to report this incident which I consider a hoax. A man has just called on the telephone and insisted on talking to me immediately. When informed that it was impossible, he gave the following message just brought to me. [*Reads note.*] " Do not put Karen Andre on the stand until I get there." No signature. [*Hands Judge note. The crash of her chair pushed back so violently that it falls, makes all eyes turn to Karen. She stands straight, eyes blazing, her calm poise shattered.*]

KAREN. I want to go on the stand right away! [*There is general commotion.*]

FLINT. May I ask why, Miss Andre?

KAREN [*Ignoring him*]. Question me now, Mr. Stevens!

STEVENS [*To Karen, much surprised*]. I'm afraid it's impossible, Miss Andre. We have to finish the examination of Mr. Jungquist.

KAREN. Then hurry! Hurry!!

FLINT. Why the hurry, Miss Andre? Whom are you expecting?

STEVENS. You don't have to answer, Miss Andre, and——

FLINT. But in view of such strange behavior——

JUDGE HEATH [*Rapping*]. Silence! I shall ask

the defendant to refrain from further interruptions!

STEVENS.  This ruling should apply to the district attorney!

JUDGE HEATH [*Raps*].  Order!  Another outbreak of this kind will find the defense counsel in contempt of court.  Proceed with the examination, Mr. Stevens.

STEVENS [*To Jungquist*].  Before this interruption, you had said that Mr. Whitfield didn't like Mr. Faulkner.  What made you say that?

JUNGQUIST.  I heard what he said one day.  Herr Faulkner was desperate for money and Herr Whitfield asked him, sarcastic, what he was going to do if his business crash.  Herr Faulkner shrugged and said " Oh, commit suicide."  Herr Whitfield looked at him, wery strange, and said, wery slow, " If you do, be sure you make a good job of it."

STEVENS.  That is all.  [*To Flint.*]  Your witness.

FLINT.  Mr. Jungquist, where were you employed before you started with Mr. Faulkner?

JUNGQUIST.  I—I worked for bank in Stockholm.

FLINT.  But you were not working there at the time immediately preceding your job with Faulkner?

JUNGQUIST.  N-no.

FLINT.  Where were you at that time?

JUNGQUIST.  I vas in prison.

FLINT.  So!  You were in jail!  On what charge?

JUNGQUIST.  Embezzlement.

FLINT. From your employer?

JUNGQUIST. Yes.

FLINT. You absconded from your bank with thirty thousand kroner, didn't you?

JUNGQUIST. Yes, I did—but Herr Faulkner helped me to get out of prison. He gave me a chance, to go straight.

FLINT. Oh—Faulkner did! He gave you a chance to go straight so that you could help him go crooked? [*Laughs, looks at* JUDGE, *who frowns.* FLINT *suddenly becomes serious.*] You have been employed by Faulkner for five years, haven't you?

JUNGQUIST. Yes.

FLINT. Did you know all that time that he was crooked?

JUNGQUIST. No, I did not.

FLINT. Do you know now that he was a swindler?

JUNGQUIST [*With the quiet dignity of a strong conviction*]. No, I do not know *that.*

FLINT. You don't, eh? And you didn't know what all those brilliant financial operations of his were?

JUNGQUIST. I knew that Herr Faulkner did what other people could not do. But I know it was not wrong.

FLINT. How did you know that?

JUNGQUIST. Because he was Herr Bjorn Faulkner.

FLINT. Oh, I see! The king could do no wrong!

JUNGQUIST. Herr Lawyer, when people like you and me meet a man like Bjorn Faulkner, we take

our hats off, and we bow, and we take orders; but
we don't ask questions.

FLINT. Splendid, my dear Mr. Jungquist! Your
devotion to your master is worthy of admiration.
You would do anything for him, wouldn't you?

JUNGQUIST. Yes.

FLINT. Are you very devoted to Miss Andre, too?

JUNGQUIST [*Significantly*]. Miss Andre served
Herr Faulkner.

FLINT. Then such a little matter as a few lies for
your master's sake would mean nothing to you?

JUNGQUIST [*With indignation*]. I have not lied,
Herr Lawyer. Herr Faulkner is dead and can-
not tell me to lie. But if I had choice, I lie for
Bjorn Faulkner rather than tell truth for you!

FLINT. For which statement I am more grateful
than you can guess, Herr Jungquist. That is all.
[JUNGQUIST *steps down.*]

STEVENS [*Solemnly*]. Karen Andre!

CLERK. Karen Andre! [KAREN *rises. She is
calm. She steps up to the stand with the poise of
a queen mounting a scaffold.*] You solemnly
swear to tell the truth, the whole truth and nothing but the truth so help you God?

KAREN. That's useless. I'm an atheist.

JUDGE HEATH. The witness has to affirm, regara-
less.

KAREN. I affirm!

STEVENS. What is your name?

KAREN. Karen Andre.

STEVENS. What was your last position?

KAREN. Secretary to Bjorn Faulkner.

STEVENS. Tell us about your first meeting.

KAREN. I saw him for the first time in his office, in Stockholm. He was alone. I had come in answer to his advertisement for a stenographer. It was my first job.

STEVENS. How did Faulkner greet you?

KAREN. He got up and didn't say a word. Just stood and looked at me. No one could stand his gaze very long; I didn't know whether I wanted to kneel—or slap his face. I didn't do either. I just told him why I had come.

STEVENS. Did he engage you then?

KAREN. He said I was too young and he didn't like me. But he threw a stenographer's pad at me and said, "Get down to work—I'm in a hurry." And I did.

STEVENS. And you worked all day?

KAREN. All day. He dictated as fast—almost faster—than he could talk. He didn't give me time to say a word. He disliked everything I did. He didn't smile once and he never took his eyes off me. He acted as if he were cracking a whip over an animal he wanted to break.

STEVENS. What happened when you had finished?

KAREN. When I finished, I told him I was quitting. He looked at me and did not answer. I put on my things and started out. He tapped on his desk once. I stopped. After a moment, he said quietly, "Tomorrow at nine—here." I went out without a word. That night I could not sleep

—his eyes were always on me.   The next morning I was in his office—at nine.

STEVENS.   And you worked, and planned, and rose to success together?

KAREN.   Yes.

STEVENS.   Can you tell us the extent of Faulkner's personal fortune at the height of his success?

KAREN.   He had no personal fortune.   He always said that the world belonged to him who could use it.   So he took what he wanted.   In business, when he owed money to one of his companies, it was crossed off the books and charged to the accounts of several other concerns.   And thus he balanced his books.   It was very simple.

STEVENS.   Why did a man of Mr. Faulkner's genius resort to such methods?

KAREN.   He wanted to build a gigantic net, a net over the whole world,—and he wanted to build it fast—in his lifetime.

STEVENS.   When did Mr. Faulkner's business difficulties start?

KAREN.   Over a year ago.

STEVENS.   Tell us about it.

KAREN.   All his corporations had begun to need money at about the same time.   So we could no longer transfer a charge from one concern to another without throwing the other into bankruptcy and thus revealing the weakness of our whole financial position.

STEVENS.   What did you do?

KAREN.   A twenty-five million dollar loan was

necessary. We tried to get it from the Whitfield Investment Corporation. But Whitfield refused it —until his daughter came into the picture.

STEVENS. How did that happen?

KAREN. Bjorn met her at a party. She soon made it obvious that she was greatly interested in him and he kept up the acquaintance—for diplomatic reasons. Then, one day, Bjorn came to me, and I'd never seen him pale before, and he said: "Karen, we have only one piece of collateral left and you're holding it. You'll have to let me borrow it for a while." I said: "Certainly. What is it?" He said it was himself. I asked: "For Nancy Whitfield?" and he nodded. I didn't answer at once—it wasn't very easy. Finally I said: "All right, Bjorn."

STEVENS. Had Mr. Faulkner proposed to Miss Whitfield?

KAREN. No. She had proposed to him.

STEVENS. How do you know that?

KAREN. He told me. She took him for a drive, stopped on a lonely road, turned to him point-blank and said: "What's the use of pretending. I want you and you know it. You don't want me and I know that. But I have the price." He asked: "And what is the price?" She said: "A certain twenty-five million dollar loan you'll need to save your business."

NANCY LEE [*Jumps up, trembling with indignation, hysterical*]. It's a lie! A shameless lie! How can you——

JUDGE HEATH [*Striking his gavel*]. Quiet, please! Anyone disturbing the proceedings will be asked to leave the courtroom!

STEVENS. What was Mr. Faulkner's answer to that, Miss Andre?

KAREN. He said: "It is costing you an awful lot of money." She said: "Money has never meant anything to me." Then he said: "Will you always remember that it's a business deal?" And she answered: "You'll have your money and I'll have you." Such was the bargain. [NANCY *protests.*]

STEVENS [*Looks at Whitfield*]. Was Mr. Whitfield eager to accept that bargain?

KAREN. Bjorn said he thought Mr. Whitfield would have a stroke when he heard about it. But Miss Whitfield insisted. She always had her way.

STEVENS. In other words, Faulkner sold himself as his last security?

KAREN. Yes.

STEVENS. Did you resent that marriage?

KAREN. No, we had always faced our business as a war. And when any war reaches a crisis, some one has to be sacrificed. The time for my sacrifice had come. But it was harder for him than for me.

STEVENS. Then why did Mr. Faulkner dismiss you two weeks after his wedding?

KAREN. He was forced to do that. Whitfield refused to advance the money until it was done.

STEVENS. What reason did he offer?

KAREN. It was Miss Whitfield's ultimatum. **I had** to be discharged.

STEVENS [*Looks at Whitfield*]. And did Mr. Whitfield grant the loan after you were dismissed?

KAREN. No, Bjorn took it.

STEVENS. How did he take it?

KAREN. By forging Mr. Whitfield's signatures on twenty-five million dollars' worth of securities.

STEVENS. How do you know that?

KAREN [*Calmly*]. I helped him to do it. [*Reaction in the courtroom.* STEVENS *is taken aback;* FLINT *chuckles*.]

STEVENS. Did this twenty-five million help Mr. Faulkner?

KAREN. Only temporarily. Bjorn had stretched his credit to the utmost—and there was no more to be had.

STEVENS. How did Mr. Faulkner take this situation?

KAREN. He knew it was the end.

STEVENS. What were his plans?

KAREN. You don't find men like Bjorn Faulkner cringing before a bankruptcy commission. And you don't find them locked in jail.

STEVENS. And the alternative?

KAREN. He wasn't afraid of the world. He had come into it as its master. He was going to leave it when and how he pleased. He was——

REGAN [*Running down aisle of auditorium*]. Karen! Stop! I phoned you to wait for me! [REGAN *is stopped by Bailiff.*]

FLINT. Regan! Larry Regan!

KAREN [*Rises*]. Larry! You promised to stay away!

JUDGE [*Raps*]. What is the meaning of this?

REGAN [*Who is being held by Bailiff*]. Karen, you don't understand!

KAREN [*To Judge*]. Your Honor! I demand that this man may not be allowed to testify!

FLINT. Why not, Miss Andre?

JUDGE. Silence, order!

MAGDA [*From aisle in auditorium*]. That's the man I see kiss her! That's the man—the sinner!

JUDGE. Admit him. [REGAN *comes to Judge's desk.*]

KAREN. Your Honor! This man loves me! He'll do anything to save me! He'll lie! Don't believe a word he says! [*She breaks off abruptly, looks at Regan defiantly.*]

REGAN [*Slowly, calmly*]. Karen, your sacrifice is useless!

KAREN. What do you mean?

REGAN. Faulkner is dead!

KAREN. Dead!

FLINT. You're on trial for his murder—didn't you know he was dead?

REGAN. No, she didn't know it! When she was arrested for Faulkner's murder, he was still alive!

KAREN. But he is alive!

REGAN. No, Karen.
KAREN. He's alive! [*She seizes the lapels of his coat hysterically.*] You're lying to me! Not Bjorn! Not Bjorn! He's waiting for me—I don't believe it!—I won't believe it! [*She breaks into a violent scream, pounding Larry frantically on the chest, as the curtain falls.*]

CURTAIN

# ACT III

*Same scene as Acts One and Two. The Court session is ready to open. Karen is brought in. Her head is bowed, her arms hanging limply. She is calm—a dead, indifferent calm. Her manner is still composed; but it is a broken person that faces us now. Her clothes are simple to an extreme. The Bailiff speaks.*

BAILIFF. Court attention! [JUDGE HEATH *enters. Everybody rises.*] Superior Court Number Eleven of the State of New York. The Honorable Judge William Heath presiding. [JUDGE HEATH *sits.* CLERK *raps and everybody resumes his seat.*]

JUDGE HEATH. The people of the State of New York versus Karen Andre.

STEVENS [*Rises*]. Ready, your Honor.

FLINT [*Rises*]. If your Honor please, I want to report that I have issued a warrant for Larry Regan's arrest, as he is obviously an accomplice in this murder. But he has disappeared. He was last seen with the defense counsel and I would like to——

REGAN [*Coming down aisle of auditorium*]. Who's disappeared? Keep your shirt on! What do you suppose I appeared for, just to give you

guys a thrill? You don't have to issue any war-
rants! I'll stay here. If she's guilty, I'm guilty.
[*He sits down at the defense table. He looks at
Karen encouragingly. She does not pay any attention to him.*]

JUDGE HEATH. The defense may proceed.

STEVENS [*Rises*]. Karen Andre. [KAREN *gets up
and walks to the stand. Her grace and poise are
gone. The movement is an obvious effort to
her.*] Miss Andre, when you took the stand yesterday, did you know the whole truth about this
case?

KAREN [*Faintly*]. No.

STEVENS. In view of certain circumstances which
have arisen, do you wish to retract any of your
testimony?

KAREN. No.

STEVENS. When you first took the stand, did you
intend to shield anyone?

KAREN. Yes.

STEVENS. Whom?

KAREN. Bjorn Faulkner.

STEVENS. Do you still find it necessary to protect
him?

KAREN [*Speaking with great effort*]. No—it's not
necessary—any more.

STEVENS. Do you still claim that Bjorn Faulkner
committed suicide?

KAREN. No. [*Forcefully*] Bjorn Faulkner did
not commit suicide. He was murdered. [*To
jury.*] I didn't kill him. Please, believe me.

[ 63 ]

Not for my sake—I don't care what you do to me now—but because you cannot let *his* murder remain unpunished! I'll tell you the whole truth. I've lied at the inquest. I've lied to my own attorney. [*To Judge.*] I was going to lie here. But everything I told you so far has been true. Now I'll tell you the rest.

STEVENS. When court adjourned yesterday, you were about to tell us about Mr. Faulkner's way out of his difficulties.

KAREN. I told you he was going to leave the world when and how he pleased. But I didn't mean that he was to kill himself. [*To jury.*] I did push a man's body off the penthouse. But that body was dead before I touched it. It was not Bjorn Faulkner.

STEVENS. Please explain this to us, Miss Andre.

KAREN. Bjorn wanted to be reported as dead. But he did not want any searches or investigations afterwards. So he decided to stage a suicide, and then disappear. I was to go with him. He had the plan in mind for a long time. He kept ten million dollars of the Whitfield loan for the purpose. But we needed someone to help us—someone who could not be connected with Bjorn in any way. There was only one such person we knew: Larry Regan.

STEVENS. What made you believe that Regan would help in so dangerous an undertaking?

KAREN. He loved me.

STEVENS. And he agreed to help you in *spite of that?*

KAREN. He agreed *because* of that.

STEVENS. What was the plan, Miss Andre?

KAREN. Regan was to get a corpse. On the night of January sixteenth, Lefty O'Toole, a gunman, was shot by rival gangsters. Regan stole his body. O'Toole's height, measurements and hair were the same as Bjorn's. [*To jury.*] He was the man I pushed off the penthouse.

STEVENS. Was that the extent of Mr. Regan's help?

KAREN. No. Regan used to be an air pilot—and he was to get an airplane and take Bjorn to South America. That day, January sixteenth, Bjorn transferred the ten millions to three banks in Buenos Aires, under the assumed name of Ragnar Hedin. A month later, I was to meet him at the Hotel Continental in Buenos Aires. Until then, the three of us were not to communicate with each other. No matter what happened, we were not to reveal the secret.

STEVENS. Tell us what happened on January sixteenth, Miss Andre.

KAREN [*Pauses*]. Bjorn came to my house that night. I'll never forget his smile when he stepped out of the elevator. He loved danger. We had dinner together. Then we went to Regan's place. He had O'Toole's body dressed in traveling clothes, with gray overcoat and hat. The three of us drove back to my house, with the body.

Bjorn wanted to be seen entering the building. [*To jury.*] So I didn't use my key—I rang the bell. We were dressed formally to make it look like a gay party. Bjorn and Regan supported the body as if he were a drunken friend. The wife of the night janitor opened the door. Then we went up in the elevator.

STEVENS. And then what happened?

KAREN [*Pauses*]. Bjorn exchanged clothes with the corpse. He wrote the letter, and propped it up on the center table where anyone could find it. The three of us had a drink—then they carried the body out and left it leaning against the parapet. Then—then, we said good-bye. [*Karen's voice is not trembling; she is not playing for sympathy; only the slightest effort in her words betrays the pain of these memories.*] Bjorn was to go first. He went down in the elevator. I stood and watched the needle of the indicator moving. Then it stopped. He was gone.

STEVENS. And then?

KAREN. Regan followed him a few minutes later. They were to meet ten miles out of the city, where Regan had left his plane. I stayed alone for an hour. The penthouse was silent. I didn't want to wait out in the garden—with the body. I lay on the bed in my room. There was a clock by the bed and it ticked in the darkness. I waited. When an hour passed, I knew the plane had taken off—that Bjorn and Regan were on their way to South America. I got up, [*Pauses*] I tore my dress—to make it look like a struggle. Then, I went to the garden. I looked down, the world seemed so far away. Then I took my gun and fired a shot into the air—[*To Stevens*] to explain the gun wound in O'Toole's body—if it were discovered. I must have been nervous, I forgot all about the finger prints. Then, I dropped the gun, and pushed the body over. I thought all of Bjorn's troubles went with it. I didn't know that —his life went, too.

STEVENS. That is all, Miss Andre.

FLINT [*Rises and comes close to her*]. Miss Andre —you said that you lied at the inquest———

KAREN. Yes.

FLINT. And you lied to your attorney———

KAREN. Yes.

FLINT. And the story you have just told us here— is entirely different from the one you came into court prepared to tell?

KAREN. It is.

FLINT. Then why should we believe a word of it? How are we to know when you are lying and when you are telling the truth?

STEVENS [*Rises*]. Objection, your Honor.

JUDGE HEATH. Sustained.

FLINT. Now, tell us, Miss Andre, didn't Mr. Faulkner have a clear conception of the difference between right and wrong?

KAREN. Bjorn never thought of things as right or wrong. To him it was only: you can or you can't. He always could.

FLINT. And yourself? Didn't you object to helping him in all his swindles?

KAREN. To me, it was only: he wants or he doesn't.

FLINT. You loved Bjorn Faulkner?

KAREN. Yes.

FLINT. Such as he was?

KAREN. *Because* he was such as he was.

FLINT. *Exactly,* Miss Andre. Now what would you do if a woman were to take away from you the man you worshipped so insanely? If she changed the ruthless brute you loved into her own ideal of an upright man? Would you still love him?

STEVENS [*Rises*]. Your Honor! We object!

JUDGE HEATH. Objection sustained.

KAREN. But I want to answer. I want the district attorney to know that he is insulting Bjorn Faulkner's memory.

FLINT. You do? But you thought nothing of insulting him while he was alive by dividing your love with a gangster?

REGAN [*Jumping up*]. Why, you lousy!——
[STEVENS *rises*.]

KAREN [*Calmly*]. Don't, Larry. [REGAN *sits down reluctantly*.] You're mistaken, Mr. Flint. Regan loved me. I didn't love him.

FLINT. And he didn't demand your love for his help?

KAREN. He demanded nothing.

FLINT. You didn't ask him to help you take revenge on your first lover?

KAREN. No!

FLINT. Why so particular, Miss Andre? Is there much difference between a swindler and a gangster?

STEVENS [*Rises*]. We object!

JUDGE HEATH. Sustained.

FLINT. You said you were the only one who knew all the details of Faulkner's swindling activities?

KAREN. Yes.

FLINT. You had enough information to send him to jail at any time?

KAREN. I'd never do that!

FLINT. But you *could,* if you'd wanted to?

KAREN. I suppose so.

FLINT. Well, Miss Andre, isn't that the explanation of Faulkner's visits to you after his marriage? He had reformed, he wanted to avoid a crash. But *you* held it over his head. You could expose him and ruin him and before he made good for his crimes. Which was it that held him in your hands? *Love* or *fear?*

KAREN. Bjorn never knew the meaning of the word *fear.*

FLINT. Miss Andre, who knew about that transfer of ten million dollars to Buenos Aires?

KAREN. Bjorn, myself and Regan.

FLINT. Not just yourself and Regan alone? With your knowledge of Faulkner's business, and your ability to forge his name, could not you and Regan alone have transferred that money?

KAREN. That would not have been necessary. Bjorn would have given me the money had I asked for it.

FLINT. Now, Miss Andre, Bjorn Faulkner kept you in extravagant luxury?

KAREN. Yes.

FLINT. You hated to change your mode of living? You hated to see him turn his fortune over to his investors? To see him poor?

KAREN. No one was ever to see him poor.

FLINT. No! Of course not! Because you and your gangster lover were going to murder him and get the ten million no one knew about!

STEVENS [*Rises*]. Your Honor! We object!

JUDGE HEATH. Sustained.

FLINT. You've heard it testified that Faulkner had no reason to commit suicide——that his marriage to Miss Whitfield had given him the first happiness he'd ever known. And you hated him for that happiness! Didn't you?

KAREN. You don't understand Bjorn Faulkner.

FLINT. Well, maybe I don't understand *him*. But let's see if I understand *you*. You formed a partnership with a swindler the first day you met him. With him you defrauded thousands of investors the world over. You cultivated a friendship with a notorious gangster. You helped in a twenty-five million dollar forgery. This you told us proudly, flaunting your defiance of all sense of honesty.

And you don't expect us to believe you capable of murder?

KAREN [*Very calmly*].   You're wrong, Mr. Flint. I *am* capable of murder—for Bjorn Faulkner's sake.

FLINT.   That is all, Miss Andre.   [KAREN *walks back to her seat at the defense table, calmly, indifferently.*]

STEVENS.   Lawrence Regan!

CLERK.   Lawrence Regan.   [REGAN *takes the stand.*]   You solemnly swear to tell the truth, the whole truth and nothing but the truth so help you God?

REGAN.   I do.

STEVENS [*Rises*].   What is your name?

REGAN.   Lawrence Regan.

STEVENS [*With a little hesitation*].   What—is your occupation?

REGAN [*Calmly, lifting one ironic eyebrow*].   Unemployed.

STEVENS.   How long have you known Karen Andre?

REGAN.   Five months.

STEVENS.   Where did you meet her?

REGAN.   In Faulkner's office.   I went to—to do some " business " with him.   I gave up the business, when I met his secretary.

STEVENS.   How did you happen to become friendly with Miss Andre?

REGAN.   The first meeting wasn't exactly friendly. She wouldn't let me in to see Mr. Faulkner.   She said I had enough money—to buy orchids by the pound—and I had no business with her boss. I said I'd think it over—and went. I thought it over. Only, I didn't think of the business. I thought of her. The next day I sent her a pound of orchids. That's how it started.

STEVENS. Did you know Miss Andre loved Mr. Faulkner?

REGAN. What of it? I knew it was hopeless for me. But I couldn't help it.

STEVENS. You never expected Miss Andre to share your feelings?

REGAN. No.

STEVENS. You never made any attempt to force them upon her?

REGAN. Do you have to know all that?

STEVENS. I'm afraid we do.

REGAN. I kissed her—once—by force. It was the night of Faulkner's wedding. She was alone—so unhappy. I didn't want her to know that I——But she knew. She told me it was no use. We've never mentioned it since.

STEVENS. When did Miss Andre first tell you of Faulkner's plans to escape to South America?

REGAN. About two weeks before we pulled it.

STEVENS. Was "Lefty O'Toole" one of your men?

REGAN. No.

STEVENS. Were you connected with his murder in any way?

REGAN. No—I'm sorry.

STEVENS [*With a little hesitation*]. You actually had no definite knowledge of his planned murder?

REGAN. No. I just had a way of guessing.

STEVENS. What happened on the night of January sixteenth?

REGAN. It all worked out as Miss Andre has told you. But she only knows half the story. I know the rest.

STEVENS. Tell us what happened after you left the penthouse.

REGAN. I left ten minutes after Faulkner. He had taken my car, to cover up his identity. I had one of my men leave another car for me at the door. I stepped on it—full speed.

STEVENS. Where did you go?——

REGAN. To Meadow Lane—ten miles out, in Kings County. I had left my plane there earlier in the evening. Faulkner was to get there first and wait for me. We were to leave at once for South America.

STEVENS. What time did you get there?

REGAN. About midnight. There was a bright moon I remember. I turned off the road and I could see tire tracks in the mud—where Faulkner's car had passed. I drove out into the lane. Then, I thought I'd lose my mind: the plane was gone.

STEVENS. What did you do?

REGAN. I searched for that plane for two hours. Faulkner's car was there—where we had agreed to hide it. It was empty, lights turned off, the

keys in the switch. I saw tracks on the ground—
where the plane had taken off. But Faulkner
wasn't a pilot—he couldn't fly the plane himself.

STEVENS. Were there any clues to this mystery?

REGAN. Yes, one. A car I found hidden in the
brush.

STEVENS [*Pauses*]. What kind of a car?

REGAN. A big black sedan.

STEVENS. And then what did you do?

REGAN. I wanted to know whose car it was, so I
crawled in the back seat and settled down to wait.

STEVENS. How long did you have to wait?

REGAN. The rest of that night.

STEVENS. And then?

REGAN. Then the owner came back. I saw him
coming. His face looked queer. He had no hat.
His clothes were wrinkled and grease-spotted.

STEVENS. What did you do?

REGAN. I pretended I was asleep in the back seat.
I watched him. He approached the car; opened
the door. Then, he saw me. He gave a start as
if he'd been struck.

STEVENS. Then, what did you do?

REGAN. I awakened, stretched, rubbed my eyes,
and said: "Oh, it's you?" He asked: "Who
are you?" I said: "My name's Larry Regan—
you may have heard it. I was in a little trouble
and had to hide out for a while. And finding this
car here was quite a convenience." He said:
"That's too bad, but I'll have to ask you to get
out. I'm in a hurry."

STEVENS. Did you get out?

REGAN. No. I stretched again and asked: "What's the hurry?" He said: "None of your business." I smiled and said I would like to have the whole story.

STEVENS. What did he say?

REGAN. At first he said nothing. He took out a check book and looked at me. I shrugged and looked at him. Then, he asked: "Would five thousand dollars be enough?" I said: "It'll do. Lawrence Regan's the name." He wrote out the check. Here it is. [REGAN *produces a check and hands it to Stevens. Reaction in the courtroom.*]

STEVENS. I offer this check in evidence! [*He passes the check to the Clerk.* CLERK *glances at it and gives a start.*]

FLINT. What's all this nonsense? Who was the man——?

STEVENS. Who was the man, Mr. Regan?

REGAN. The clerk can read that check to you.

STEVENS [*To Clerk*]. Kindly read the check.

CLERK [*Reads*]. "Pay to the order of Lawrence Regan the sum of five thousand dollars. Signed: John Graham Whitfield." [*Uproar in courtroom.* WHITFIELD *jumps to his feet.*]

WHITFIELD. Why, it's an outrage! [JUDGE HEATH *raps.*]

FLINT [*Examines the check*]. I demand to see that check!

STEVENS. We offer this check in evidence!

FLINT. Objection!

JUDGE HEATH. Objection overruled. Admitted in evidence. [FLINT *gives check to Clerk*.]

STEVENS. What did you do after you received this check, Mr. Regan?

REGAN. I drew my gun and stuck it in his ribs, and said: " Now, you lousy cur, what did you do with Faulkner? "

WHITFIELD [*Rises*]. Your Honor! Is this man to be allowed to make such statements——

JUDGE HEATH [*Raps*]. The witness is allowed to testify. If it is proved to be perjury, he will suffer the consequences. Proceed, Mr. Stevens.

STEVENS. What did he answer, Mr. Regan?

REGAN. At first, he muttered: " I don't know what you're talking about." But I jammed the gun harder and I said: " I've no time to waste. Where did you take him? "

STEVENS. Did you get any information out of him?

REGAN. Not a word. I talked and threatened. It was no use. I let him go. [*To Whitfield*.] I knew I could always get him. I didn't want to kill him—yet.

STEVENS. Then did you try to find Faulkner?

REGAN. I didn't lose a second. I rushed home, jumped into some flying clothes, grabbed another plane—and flew to Buenos Aires. I searched. I advertised in the papers, but got no answer. No one called at the banks for the ten millions we transferred under the name of Ragnar Hedin.

STEVENS. Did you try to communicate about this with Miss Andre?

REGAN. No. We had promised to stay away from each other for a month. And she had been arrested—for Faulkner's murder. I laughed when I read that. But I couldn't say a word—not to betray Faulkner if he were still alive. I waited.

STEVENS. What were you waiting for?

REGAN. For the month to pass—February sixteenth. I went to the Hotel Continental in Buenos Aires and I set my teeth and waited every minute of every hour of that last day. He didn't come.

STEVENS. Then?

REGAN. Then I knew he was dead. I came back to New York. I started a search for my plane. We found it—yesterday.

STEVENS. Where did you find it?

REGAN. In a deserted valley in New Jersey, twenty miles from Meadow Lane. [*To Whitfield.*] I recognized the plane by the engine number. It had been landed and fire set to it.

STEVENS. Was the plane—empty?

REGAN. No. I found the body of a man in it.

STEVENS. Could you identify him?

REGAN. No one could. It was nothing but a burned skeleton. But the height was the same. It was Faulkner. [STEVENS *looks at Whitfield.*] I examined the body—or what was left of it. I found two bullet wounds in the bones. One through the right hand; the other over the heart. He must have been disarmed first, shot through the hand, then, murdered, defenseless, straight through the heart.

STEVENS [*After a little pause*]. That's all, Mr. Regan. Your witness.

FLINT. Just what is your—*business*, Mr. Regan?

REGAN. I have refused that information to others —it would seem so partial if I told only you.

FLINT. Mr. Regan, what do you do when prospective clients refuse to pay you protection?

REGAN. I'm legally allowed not to understand what you're talking about.

FLINT. Then I will try to make it clear. May I question you as to whether you read the newspapers?

REGAN. You may. [*He is manicuring his nails.*]

FLINT. Well?

REGAN. Question me.

FLINT. Will you kindly state whether you read newspapers?

REGAN. Occasionally.

FLINT. Did you happen to read that when Mr. James Sutton Vance Jr. refused to pay protection to— [STEVENS *rises and sits.*] a certain gangster, his magnificent country house in Westchester was destroyed by an explosion, just after the guests left, barely missing a wholesale slaughter? What was that, a coincidence?

REGAN [*Violently sarcastic*]. A remarkable coincidence, Mr. Flint!—Just after the guests left.

FLINT. Did you read that when Mr. Van Dorn refused to——

STEVENS [*Rises*]. We object, your Honor! Such questions are irrelevant!

JUDGE HEATH. Sustained.

FLINT. So you had no ill feeling towards Mr. Faulkner for the—failure of your—business—with him?

REGAN. No.

FLINT. Now, Mr. Lawrence Regan, what would you do if someone were to take this woman you love so much, and throw her aside, merely because he had found someone else with more money?

REGAN. I'd cut his throat with a dull saw.

FLINT [*Taken back*]. You would?

REGAN. I would!

FLINT. And yet you expect us to believe that you, Larry Regan, gangster, outlaw, scum of the underworld, would step aside with a grand gesture and again throw this same woman you love back into the arms of this same man?

STEVENS [*Rises*]. Your Honor! We——

REGAN [*Interrupts him by turning to Flint and saying very calmly, very earnestly*]. I loved her.

FLINT. You did? Then why did you allow Faulkner to visit her after his marriage?

REGAN. Just a rare privilege.

FLINT. You two didn't hold a blackmail plot over his head?

REGAN. Got any proof of that?

FLINT. Her association with you is the best proof!

STEVENS. Objection!

JUDGE HEATH. Sustained.

FLINT. How did you kill Faulkner in the penthouse that night?

STEVENS. Objection.

JUDGE HEATH. Sustained.

FLINT. You deny having any part in Faulkner's murder?

REGAN. I do.

FLINT. You deny you were an accomplice to that murder?

REGAN. I do.

FLINT. But you admit knowledge of the fantastic plot which Miss Andre has just described?

REGAN. I do.

FLINT. To what extent did you participate?

REGAN. Mr. Flint, I merely provided the corpse.

FLINT [*Surprised at his frankness*]. And nothing else?

REGAN. Nothing else.

FLINT. Exhibit B, please. [CLERK *hands him the gun.*] Do you recognize this gun?

REGAN [*Taking gun*]. No.

FLINT. Perhaps I should refresh your memory. This is the gun found in the penthouse—the gun Miss Andre claims she fired in the air—the gun she claims was hers. Now do you recognize it?

REGAN. No.

FLINT. Affidavit, please. [*Gets it from his secretary.*] I have here an affidavit which states that a 32 calibre pistol No. cc3490 was sold by a store in New Jersey to Lawrence Regan.

STEVENS [*Rises. To Flint*]. Just a minute, Mr. Flint. I would like to look at that affidavit.

REGAN [*Examining gun*]. There is no cc3490 on

[ 80 ]

this gun, Mr. District Attorney. [*Gives gun to Flint.*]

FLINT. No! Did you ever hear of the heat test?

REGAN. No.

FLINT. The number on this gun has been filed off; but when heated red hot, it still discloses the serial number cc3490. [*He returns the gun to the Clerk.*]

STEVENS [*Handing the affidavit to Flint*]. This is satisfactory, Mr. Flint.

FLINT. Submitted in evidence.

JUDGE. Accepted—Exhibit F.

FLINT. You admit being with Mr. Faulkner and Miss Andre in the penthouse on the night of January sixteenth?

REGAN. I do.

FLINT. Then perhaps you will tell us where is your other accomplice—the man who played the drunk?

REGAN. "Lefty" O'Toole? I can give you his exact address: Evergreen Cemetery, Whitfield Family Memorial, which is the swankiest place poor "Lefty's" ever been.

FLINT. Now, let me get this clear: you claim that the man buried in Evergreen Cemetery is "Lefty" O'Toole?

REGAN. Yes, and the same corpse that was thrown from the penthouse.

FLINT. And the man you found in the burned plane was Bjorn Faulkner?

REGAN. Yes.

FLINT. What is to prove that it isn't the other way

round? Supposing you did steal O'Toole's body? What's to prove that you didn't stage that fantastic thing yourself—that you didn't plant the airplane and the body in New Jersey and then come here today with this wild story, in a desperate attempt to save Miss Andre? You've heard her tell us that you'd do anything for her; that you'd lie for her—murder for her.

STEVENS [*Rises*]. We object, your Honor!

JUDGE HEATH. Objection sustained.

FLINT. Where's your real proof, Mr. Regan?

REGAN [*He looks straight at Flint for a second. When he speaks, his manner is a startling contrast to his former arrogance and irony; it is simple, sincere; it is almost majestic in its earnestness*]. Mr. Flint, you're a district attorney and I—well, you know what I am. We both have a lot of dirty work to do. Such happens to be life—or most of it. But do you think we're both so low that if something passes us to which one kneels, we no longer have eyes to see it? I loved her; she loved Faulkner. That's our only proof.

FLINT. That's all, Mr. Regan. [REGAN *returns to the defense table.* KAREN *looks at him. She extends her hand. He shakes it. He sits down.*]

STEVENS [*Rises*]. Your Honor. The defense rests——

JUDGE HEATH. Any witnesses in rebuttal?

FLINT [*Rises*]. Your Honor if you please, the prosecution has one. Roberta Van Rensselaer!

CLERK. Roberta Van Rensselaer! [*She flounces*

*down the aisle and up to the witness stand.*] You solemnly swear to tell the truth, the whole truth and nothing but the truth so help you God?

ROBERTA. Certainly. Why not?

FLINT. Your name?

ROBERTA. Real, or professional?

FLINT. Both, if you don't mind.

ROBERTA. I don't mind. My real name is Ruby O'Toole. But if we should ever get friendly, don't call me " Ruby "—I hate that name.

FLINT. But professionally known as Roberta Van Rensselaer?

ROBERTA. That's my nom de plume—— I'm a terpsichorean.

FLINT. You mean you dance?

ROBERTA. That's the common name for it.

FLINT. Where were you last employed?

ROBERTA. At the Club Chez O'Toole. No cover charge.

FLINT. Who was your employer?

ROBERTA. The owner—George " Lefty " O'Toole.

FLINT. Were you related to him?

ROBERTA. No—I was his wife.

FLINT. I see. Now tell me, do you know Larry Regan?

ROBERTA [*Indifferently*]. I've met the rat.

FLINT. I take it you haven't much affection for him. [*Looks at Regan.*]

ROBERTA. If we were cast off together on a lonely island, it would still be lonely.

FLINT. Why do you dislike him?

ROBERTA [*Gritting her teeth*]. Because he killed
" Lefty " O'Toole!

STEVENS [*Rises*]. We object, your Honor.

JUDGE HEATH. Strike it out.

FLINT. You must forego your personal opinions,
Miss Van Rensselaer, and confine yourself to the
facts—of your personal knowledge. Did O'Toole
and Regan do business together?

ROBERTA. No. If " Lefty " had stooped that
low, he would have broke his back.

FLINT. Then would you say that they were rivals?

ROBERTA. Larry might say so, but " Lefty " just
considered him an amusement—like golf or fish-
ing.

FLINT. When did you see Regan last?

ROBERTA. See him—or hear from him?

FLINT. See him.

ROBERTA. About a month before " Lefty " was
rubbed out. Regan came over to the club one
night to see " Lefty," and " Lefty " had me sit
at the table and listen. He always did that because Regan had been trying to muscle in.

FLINT. And what did Regan want that night?

ROBERTA. He said he wanted to sell out.

FLINT. Did that surprise you?

ROBERTA. You could have carried me out in a
spoon.

FLINT. Was O'Toole interested in the proposi-
tion?

ROBERTA. No. He said that Larry don't sit long
enough in one place to get a shine on his pants.

FLINT. Why did he want to sell out?

ROBERTA. His story was he's leaving the country for good. He described a jane he had on the run —and a lot of important money she's going to have—and how they were going to South America and put the Equator between them and the income tax boys.

FLINT. Did he mention who the woman was?

ROBERTA. No—but "Lefty" knew. He said it was some jane working in Faulkner's office. But it wouldn't do him any good, because Faulkner would stop him.

FLINT. What did Regan say to that?

ROBERTA. He said Faulkner was going away for good, and "Lefty" says, "You planning to erase him?" And Regan answers, "No, he's going to commit a fake suicide—and won't he be surprised when he finds it's real."

STEVENS [*Rises*]. Objection, your Honor. This is hearsay and not admissible.

JUDGE HEATH. Overruled.

STEVENS. Exception.

FLINT. Do you recall the rest of the conversation?

ROBERTA. They talked about a price for his interests and "Lefty" said he would think it over.

FLINT. When did you hear from him again?

ROBERTA. On January sixteenth. Regan phoned the house and asked for "Lefty." I put "Lefty" on the phone; and after they talked, "Lefty" said he was going out to Sands Point to meet Regan and settle the deal.

FLINT. And he left the house to meet Regan?

ROBERTA. Yes—to go to Long Island. He was put on the spot on the Queensboro Bridge.

FLINT. He was killed that same night?

ROBERTA. Yes, and an hour after, his body disappeared.

FLINT [*To Stevens*]. Your witness.

STEVENS. You are the widow of George O'Toole?

ROBERTA. Yes.

STEVENS. And you admit that you hate Lawrence Regan?

ROBERTA. I swear to it.

STEVENS. Haven't you allowed that fact to influence your testimony?

ROBERTA. How do you mean?

STEVENS. I mean that you are here to get revenge, and that you relate things which you know nothing about. For instance, you said that Regan was losing money. How could you possibly know that?

ROBERTA. We kept better books for Regan than he kept for the Government.

STEVENS. You said your husband met his death on the sixteenth of January.

ROBERTA. Yes.

STEVENS. And it is rumored that he was " put on the spot " by rival gangsters.

ROBERTA. Yes, and the man who did it was——

STEVENS. Please confine your answers to the questions put to you. You believe he was killed by a rival?

[ 86 ]

ROBERTA. It couldn't possibly have been anyone else——

STEVENS. But you didn't consider Regan a rival. Isn't that what you said?

ROBERTA. You don't have to consider a skunk your rival just because you try to keep him off your farm.

STEVENS. That is all.

ROBERTA [*Half rises*]. Killing " Lefty " O'Toole was the dirtiest trick——

STEVENS. That is all, Miss Van Rensselaer.

ROBERTA [*As she rises*]. It *was* dirty, Judge. [*She exits by the jury box and gives the jurors a quick nod and smile.*]

JUDGE HEATH. Any more witnesses?

STEVENS [*Rises*]. Your Honor, please, I would like to recall John Graham Whitfield. [WHITFIELD *rises quickly and walks to the stand hurriedly, resolutely.*] Mr. Whitfield, have you any objection if I ask for a court order to examine the body in Evergreen Cemetery?

WHITFIELD. I have no objection, Mr. Stevens— but that body has been cremated.

STEVENS. Oh! Cremated! Why was that done, Mr. Whitfield?

WHITFIELD. The body was in such a condition that it seemed the best thing to do.

STEVENS. And for no other reason?

WHITFIELD. Well, it's been a custom of our family for years.

STEVENS. Mr. Whitfield, where were you on the night of January sixteenth?

WHITFIELD [*Very calmly*]. I was at home.

STEVENS. Have you any witnesses to that?

WHITFIELD [*Good naturedly*]. Mr. Stevens, you must realize that I am not in the habit of providing myself with alibis. I've never had reasons to keep track of my activities and produce witnesses for them. But if you insist, I believe I spoke to my daughter—— [*Looks at Nancy Lee.*]

STEVENS [*Interrupting*]. How many cars do you own, Mr. Whitfield?

WHITFIELD. Four.

STEVENS. What are they?

WHITFIELD. One of them *is* a black sedan, as you are evidently anxious to learn. May I remind you that it isn't the only black sedan in New York City.

STEVENS [*Casually*]. You have just returned by plane from California?

WHITFIELD. Yes.

STEVENS. You flew it yourself?

WHITFIELD. Yes.

STEVENS. You're a licensed pilot, then?

WHITFIELD. I am.

STEVENS. And yet that story of Mr. Regan's, about your running away with his plane and burning it in New Jersey, is nothing but a lie in your opinion?

WHITFIELD. It is.

STEVENS [*Close to witness chair, changing his*

*manner, fiercely*]. Then who wrote that check for five thousand dollars?

WHITFIELD. I did.

STEVENS [*Astounded*]. You admit it?

WHITFIELD. I do.

STEVENS. Explain yourself.

WHITFIELD. We all know Larry Regan's profession. He had threatened my daughter. I preferred to buy him off rather than take a chance on the life of my child. So on January 6th I gave him a check for five thousand dollars.

STEVENS. You mean you gave it to him on January 16th?

WHITFIELD. No—on January 6th.

STEVENS. This check is dated January 16th.

WHITFIELD. Yes. Regan has added a one and made it the 16th.

STEVENS. You mean he changed the date?

WHITFIELD. You may call a handwriting expert and find out.

STEVENS [*Stumped*]. Kindly refrain from advising me. [*He studies him a moment.*] Your daughter and your fortune are your most cherished possessions, aren't they?

WHITFIELD. They are.

STEVENS. Then what would you do to the man who stole your money and deserted your daughter for another woman?

FLINT [*Rises*]. We object, your Honor!

JUDGE HEATH. Objection sustained.

STEVENS [*Rapidly*]. Exception. You hated Faulk-

ner! You wanted to break him! You suspected
his intentions of staging a suicide! The words
Mr. Jungquist heard you say prove it! Didn't
you?

WHITFIELD. I suspected nothing of the kind!

STEVENS. And on January sixteenth, didn't you
spend the day following Faulkner?

WHITFIELD. Certainly not!

STEVENS. Didn't you follow him as soon as he left
the penthouse that night?

WHITFIELD. No.

STEVENS. Didn't you have any particular information about Faulkner's activities at the time?

WHITFIELD. None.

STEVENS. You heard nothing unusual that day?

WHITFIELD. Not a thing.

STEVENS. You did not hear about the ten million
dollars he transferred to Buenos Aires?

WHITFIELD. I never heard of it.

JUNGQUIST [*From audience, begins to yell and
comes on stage*]. I killed him! I killed Bjorn
Faulkner! I helped *that man* to kill him! [*He
points at Whitfield.*] The whole truth, so help
me God! I didn't know! I see it now! [*He
points at Whitfield.*] He killed Faulkner! Because he lied! He knew about the ten million
dollars! Because I told him! [STEVENS *rushes
at him, whispers.*]

FLINT. Now, look here, my man, you can't——

STEVENS [*Hurriedly*]. That's all, Mr. Whitfield.

FLINT.  No questions.

[WHITFIELD *leaves the stand*.]

STEVENS.  Kindly take the stand, Mr. Jungquist. [JUNGQUIST *obeys, staggering*.]  You told Mr. Whitfield about that transfer?

JUNGQUIST [*Hysterically*].  He ask me many times about ten million—where it spent.  I did not know it was a secret.  That day—I tell him—about Buenos Aires.  That day—at noon—January sixteenth!  [JUDGE *raps*.]

WHITFIELD [*Rises*].  What kind of a frame-up is this?

FLINT [*Rises*].  Ssh——

STEVENS.  You told Whitfield?  At noon?

JUNGQUIST.  Yes, I did.  God help me!  I didn't know!  I would give my life for Herr Faulkner!  And I helped to kill him!  [*He breaks down into hysterical sobbing*.]

STEVENS  That's all.

FLINT [*Bends over him*].  Jungquist, were you alone with Mr. Whitfield when you told him?

JUNGQUIST [*Surprised*].  Yes.

FLINT.  Then it's the word of an ex-convict against John Graham Whitfield?

JUNGQUIST [*Stunned by the sudden thought, feebly*]. Yes.

FLINT.  That's all.  [JUNGQUIST *sobs*.]

JUDGE HEATH.  The Bailiff will escort Mr. Jungquist out of the courtroom.  [JUNGQUIST *is led to door by* BAILIFF.]  The defense may proceed with the closing argument.

STEVENS [*Rises and goes to jury box*]. Your
Honor! Gentlemen of the jury! In a few mo-
ments you will be called upon to decide the fate
of a woman. Her very life rests in your hands
and I am here to plead for that life. Karen
Andre has confessed here to you many question-
able things which may arouse you against her.
But she is not being tried for those things. She
is being tried only for the murder of Bjorn Faulkner, and to hold her guilty of that murder you
must convince yourselves of two things: that she
had a motive and that the evidence proves she
committed the crime. What direct evidence has
been submitted to you? Merely that Karen Andre
threw a body from a penthouse. We admit that.
But we deny that it was the body of Bjorn Faulkner.

Now what about the motive? In business, the
lives of Karen Andre and Bjorn Faulkner were
one. Think of Bjorn Faulkner. The State
claims that he had reformed his methods, that he
became a devoted husband, that he dedicated his
life to the task of saving his unfortunate investors.
Do you believe that he was the kind to renounce
his whole life and repent? If you do—she's
guilty. But have you followed the testimony?
After his marriage he did not take his wife into
his confidence, and failed to explain his absence
from her night after night. Was that the act of a
devoted husband? On January sixteenth, he absconded with ten million dollars. Was that the

act of a man trying to save his investors? When he realized that he could no longer hold off the collapse of his empire, he decided to stage a fake suicide. And to whom did he confide his plans? To his wife? No—to Karen Andre. Who was to meet him in South America? His wife? No —Karen Andre. There was every possible advantage to Karen Andre if Faulkner lived. She had no motive for killing him. We admit that Karen Andre helped Faulkner in his swindles. We admit that the story she told at the inquest was a lie. But none of these things make her a murderess! Remember this! Karen Andre loved Faulkner. That is her only defense. Is it in you to understand her? Is it in you to understand the man she loved?

Who is on trial in this case? Karen Andre? No. It's you, gentlemen of the jury, who are here on trial. It is your souls and minds and the very deepest, secret chords of your hearts that will be brought to light when your decision is rendered! And I ask you for a verdict of not guilty!

JUDGE HEATH. The District Attorney may now conclude the case.

FLINT [*Rises—to jury*]. Your Honor! Gentlemen of the jury! I am not going to appeal to your " souls," or to those " deep secret chords of your hearts "—but to your reason alone. I have no need to appeal to your sympathies, for the only things that concern you in this case are the facts. And, as I enumerate them to you, bear in mind that they are not manufactured alibis—but FACTS! [*Pause.*] Bjorn Faulkner was killed on the night of January sixteenth. He was murdered! His body was thrown from the parapet outside that penthouse by Karen Andre, and a detective from a nearby roof was an eye witness to it! *And that is a fact!* He was already dead. He had been shot in that penthouse and the recently discharged gun was found in that apartment by the police. The defense claims that he fired the gun himself in an attempted suicide. But the gun bore the finger prints of Karen Andre and of nobody else. *And that is another fact!!* That gun was the property of Larry Regan, who was in the apartment that night—although she had sworn that she had never seen him before. According to the testimony of the housekeeper, Larry Regan was her lover; and with him she had conspired to ship ten million dollars to South America. Where did they get such a sum? By forging the name of John Graham Whitfield! And that is a *fact,* a fact which Karen Andre herself has admitted here on the witness stand. Now why did they do all this? A child could give you the answer. Karen Andre hated Faulkner, because he had married another woman, and then discharged her from his office. She was determined to accomplish two things: first, avenge herself on Faulkner, and then seize his money and thus insure for herself the depraved luxury to which she had become accustomed—and both of these things she planned with her new lover, Larry Regan. And so between them they concocted this diabolically clever alibi—this confusion of corpses—this cock-and-bull story—the sheer impudence of which almost carried it to success. On January 16th, "Lefty" O'Toole was lured from his home in answer to a telephone call from Larry Regan, and was later found dead. On January 16th the money was sent to South America. On January 16th Bjorn Faulkner was shot to death and his body hurled to the sidewalks so that the condition of his body might both conceal the bullet wound and make identification difficult. And then, on the night of January 16th the body of "Lefty" O'Toole was stolen and taken in an aeroplane to New Jersey by Larry Regan and the plane and the body burned. And finally, a check for five thousand dollars was taken from John Graham Whitfield by blackmail and then the date changed in the ridiculous attempt to implicate him in the crime! THESE ARE THE FACTS IN THIS CASE, a case so strong that I can conceive of no other verdict than the one I ask you to return—MURDER IN THE FIRST DEGREE!

JUDGE HEATH [*Rises*]. Gentlemen of the jury, the Bailiff will now escort you to the jury room. I shall ask you to consider your verdict carefully: omitting all personal prejudices and sympathies. I shall ask you to adhere strictly to the evidence, and to bear in mind the gun, the finger prints on it, the admitted forgeries and the motives which may have caused this crime to be committed. You are to determine only whether Karen Andre is guilty or not guilty of the murder of Bjorn Faulkner. You may bring in a verdict of acquittal or of murder in the first degree. [*Exits to chamber. The* BAILIFF *escorts the jury out. After the jury leaves the courtroom, the stage is darkened. Then, one by one, a spotlight picks out of the darkness the different witnesses, who repeat the most significant lines of their testimony, a quick succession of contradicting statements, presenting both sides of the case, reviewing the case for the audience, giving it swift flashes of what the jury is deliberating.*]

MRS. HUTCHINS [*As the spot is put on her*]. I couldn't see his face, countin' his hat was all crooked over his eyes and his coat collar turned up.

WHITFIELD. It was a difficult undertaking, but I felt that the crash could have been prevented— had Faulkner lived.

SWEENEY. I found only *two* valuable things on this earth—My whip over the world and Karen Andre.

CHANDLER. A certain peculiarity in the handwriting led me to claim this letter *was forged*.

VAN FLEET. No lights—Karen Andre's white gown shimmering in the moonlight—a man in evening clothes—Faulkner leaning against the parapet. She pushes him with all her strength— He goes over the parapet—down into space.

KIRKLAND. It was impossible to determine—It could have been the wound or the fall.

NANCY LEE. But he realized his past mistakes. He was ready to atone for them—when I came into his life.

JUNGQUIST. I didn't know—but I see now—he killed Faulkner because he lied! He knew about the ten million dollars because I told him!

MAGDA. She asked me to put it on as hot as she can stand, and if it burned her shameless skin—she laugh like pagan she is, and say it was man kissing her wild like tiger.

ROBERTA. He left the house to meet Regan—He was put on the spot on the Queensboro Bridge.

REGAN. Do you think we're both so low that if something passes us to which one kneels, we no longer have eyes to see it? I loved her; she loved Faulkner. That's our only proof.

KAREN. You are wrong. I *am* capable of murder —for *Bjorn Faulkner's* sake! [*After the last flash, the stage remains dark for a few seconds. Then the lights come on and the jury returns into the courtroom.*]

BAILIFF. Attention of the Court! [JUDGE HEATH *enters. Everybody rises.* JUDGE HEATH *sits.* CLERK *raps and everybody resumes his seat.*] Prisoner will rise and face the jury. [KAREN *rises, head high up.*] The jury will rise and face the prisoner. Mr. Foreman, have you reached a verdict?

FOREMAN. We have!

## *NOT GUILTY VERDICT*

BAILIFF.  What say you?

FOREMAN.  Not guilty!

KAREN [*Gratefully*].  Won! Gentlemen of the jury, I thank you.

STEVENS.  Your Honor, I ask that the prisoner be discharged.

BAILIFF.  Prisoner face the court.

JUDGE.  The prisoner is discharged.  But—the Court sees no reason to thank this jury for a verdict which in my opinion is contrary to the evidence.  I shall order the names of these jurors stricken from the jury rolls for five years.  The Court stands adjourned.

CURTAIN

## *THE GUILTY VERDICT*

BAILIFF.  What say you?

FOREMAN.  Guilty!

KAREN [*Hopelessly*].  Lost!

BAILIFF.  Prisoner face the Court.

JUDGE.  It is my duty to set a date for sentence. In order to give you ample time the prisoner will be brought before me the 30th day of this month.

STEVENS.  Your Honor, I wish to file an order of appeal.

JUDGE HEATH.  And you have excellent grounds. I see no reason to thank the jury for a verdict which in my opinion is contrary to the evidence. I shall order the names of these jurors stricken from the jury rolls for five years. The Court now stands adjourned.

CURTAIN